PRAISE FOR
WHEN YOU LEAVE ME

"A twisty mystery about love, betrayal, and obsession. In a small town, everyone's a murder suspect. The ending packs a punch and remains in the reader's mind long after turning the final page. Thriller aficionados will devour this story."

—Robert Dugoni, *New York Times* bestselling author of the Tracy Crosswhite series

"A cup of hot coffee at my side, I dove into Susan Wingate's *When You Leave Me*. The coffee was cold when I reached for a sip, so enthralled I was by the storyline. Artfully constructed, melodic, and insightful, *When You Leave Me* is not just a complex, captivating mystery—it's a poignant reminder to never take love for granted."

—Christopher Rosow, author of the bestselling *False Assurances* and the Ben Porter thriller series

"Susan Wingate grabs you from the very first sentence of *When You Leave Me* and never lets you go. This thriller is a roller coaster ride of tension and suspense, delivered in punchy, elegant prose and with dialogue that provides a window into the personalities of the author's characters. You're going to love this one."

—Joseph Badal, award-winning author of *The Carnevale Conspiracy*

"What Susan Wingate does best in *When You Leave Me*, as in her previous novels, is to make human pain palpable to the reader. In this newest offering, threads of pain run through every page. On San Juan Island off the coast of Washington, a husband with dementia goes missing. Then a foot in a sneaker washes ashore amidst a rash of such grotesque discoveries. Thus begins, for Jamie Michaels, the missing man's wife, a tormented journey as she claws her way through a sea turgid with grief, guilt, and fear. Is Jamie responsible for her husband's fate? The police seem to think so, and so does she. But that, in the end, isn't the question. The real questions, as every person knows who has ever cared for a loved one with dementia, are how long must this punishment last? And how can I possibly survive it?"

—Randall Silvis, author of the critically acclaimed
Ryan DeMarco mystery series

When You Leave Me

BOOKS BY SUSAN WINGATE

The Friday Harbor Novels
The Lesser Witness
Storm Season
The Deer Effect
How the Deer Moon Hungers
When You Leave Me

The Bobby's Diner Series
Bobby's Diner
Hotter than Helen
Sacrifice at Sea

Novels
Of the Law
Way of the Wild Wood
Troubled in Paradise
The Last Maharajan

Non-Fiction
The Dementia Chronicles

Susan Wingate

When You Leave Me

DOWN&OUT
BOOKS

Down & Out Books
3959 Van Dyke Road, Suite 265
Lutz, FL 33558
DownAndOutBooks.com

The characters and events in this book are fictitious. Any similarity to real persons, living or dead, is coincidental and not intended by the author.

Cover design by Susan Wingate

ISBN: 1-64396-256-6
ISBN-13: 978-1-64396-256-6

For Bob

*"It is the extreme situation that best reveals
what we are essentially."*
—Flannery O'Connor

"And she being desolate shall sit on the ground."
—Isaiah, 3-26

The Chronicler of the San Juan Islands
Published: 8:36 AM PDT, September 21, 2020
MYSTERY FOOT WASHES ASHORE ON SOUTH BEACH

SAN JUAN COUNTY, Wash.—The San Juan County Sheriff's Office is investigating whether a shoe that washed ashore on a beach contains a human foot.

Deputies say on Friday, a woman in her fifties found what she said on the 9-1-1 call "looks like a foot inside a sneaker near Eagle Cove on South Beach."

"When we say foot, well, it's kind of iffy at this point," Det. Sgt. Rob Rimmler said Sunday. "We don't know, at this point, whether it's human and, if it's human, if it's from a male or female."

Officials aren't sure if the shoe is connected to an ongoing mystery of detached feet around Port Townsend, Washington, that have occurred during and pre-COVID-19, where five athletic shoes containing human feet have been found since August of last year. A sixth foot found in June turned out to be what officials called "a hoax" and have chosen not to give out further details. "As details might be relevant to this current investigation," officials said.

The coroner of Washington's San Juan County is trying to determine whether any of the feet belong to a footless body found along Orcas Island in March, an adult male whose estranged wife could not be located for identification. A positive identification was made by the man's neighbor. Authorities have not yet released the man's identity.

Earlier in the summer, San Juan County authorities sent out Search & Rescue for a man with dementia, who had gone missing. The sheriff's office is not confirming or denying if the shoe belongs to the missing man.

Some experts say certain extremities, like feet, often detach from bodies after being submerged in the ocean, and these feet are likely being discovered because they are in laced-up running shoes. Shoes will float but the laces can also serve as ligatures and act to accelerate detachment.

Neither are investigators saying if some feet were actually intentionally cut from the bodies or if they might have been detached due to a shark bite. Nor have investigators stated if they know where the feet are coming from or if they suspect foul play.

SEARCH & RESCUE—Then & Now

CHAPTER 1
THEN—June 20, 2020

A broken wing. A thousand feet above earth. Extreme speed. A frenzied Kingfisher, tumbling down, down, down.

People lose their keys, they lose their reading glasses, hell, they even lose their minds! People, however, do not lose their spouses. At least, they *shouldn't*.

Jamie Michaels had prayed most of the day up to the point when deputies appeared and then, after that, to herself after they finally left the house.

Two things happened the night of the book club meeting. The island where they live suffered a short but massive earthquake, and Larry went missing.

The last time the region had suffered a shocker *that* size and that close to the island was when a quake hit Cumberland, B.C. That one ranked 7.5 on the Richter scale, happening a mere five miles away if traveling a straight shot across the water from San Juan Island's westmost coastline to Vancouver Island's eastmost coastline. It had been seventy-four years ago, in 1946 since white settlers had come to Friday Harbor. In 1853, how had settlers survived a shock that size when Jamie's own home today, in 2020, had bent and creaked under this quake's fury?

* * *

"You got home when?"

Oh, God. Please Rob. I told you already.

Her skin went clammy under her clothing. "Not sure of the exact time. I didn't look at a clock." She pushed her sleeves up. She needed to check her attitude. "I was sort of upset. I searched downstairs, then upstairs, outside," she gestured, sweeping her right arm out as though featuring an amazing prize won by a guest on a ridiculous game show, "when I didn't find him in his usual spot."

Jamie and Detective Sergeant Rob Rimmler stood near the front door on a barn red porch that ran well past the length of the house, wrapped around the sides, then disappeared off in the back to a split-level section of the deck. Years of good use had worn holes in the boards but the deck, overall, was sturdy.

Rob pulled out his trademark red-checkered handkerchief from his back pocket, took two swipes, this way and that, at his nose, then re-pocketed the kerchief. The handkerchief took on its own character with a story all of its own around the island. The snot rag developed into something of lore in the years since Rimmler had landed on the island. People gamed that he used the rag to humanize situations. How can a perp feel too scared or too nervous when a cop stops his questioning, slows down, and pulls out a checkered cotton hanky, right? Hell, people imitated him as if they were the ones pulling a guy over for drunk driving or for speeding down a twenty-five-mile-per-hour road. Something Jamie had called him out for several times. Something she loathed, the speeding.

But now, Jamie wondered if his handkerchief was a ploy, a law enforcement technique. Then she kicked the idea in the butt, chalked it up to allergies, and gave him the benefit of doubt.

She couldn't count the times she'd seen the rag peeking out

of his hind pocket—at the grocery store coming up from behind him, while Rob stood on the street talking with locals in front of the movie theater, when he stopped to talk to her those times on her morning run. The rag, his companion of sorts, poking its face out like a grimy boy peeking around a father's hip, clinging to him.

Jamie wondered if he ever laundered it. He must, right?

Different types of DNA flashed across in a mental ticker tape...saliva, snot...*semen*.

She shivered.

Rob re-pocketed the rag. "You cold?" he asked.

She nodded, hoping to hurry him along.

He held a pad of paper in his left hand and took notes with the pen in his right. And although the illumination of the porch-light helped, the pen had a tiny built-in light to aid on dark nights like these. She keyed in on its beam, a gnat to a flame. Suddenly, he scratched an itch on his upper lip with the hand still holding the pen, its light jumping around the porch like a nervous sharpshooter taking shaky aim at a bullseye.

He shifted, moving from one foot to the other, tugging on his belt making his gear rattle—pepper spray, a ring of a thousand keys, the light slap of a phone coil that hooked into his shoulder mic. And when he transferred his weight, that one *frigging* loose board in the deck cried under his load.

At once, the sound made her cringe. Jamie had been wanting to replace their deck for ten years. Instead, they ended up paint-ing it red—barn red—for a more *countrified* look, Larry sug-gested. "The lesser of two evils," he'd said, with Jamie acquiesc-ing. However, within only a couple years the red faded along with the memory of why they'd thought painting instead of re-placing was a good idea. Back then, they still had an overabun-dance of cash flow. But like with everything, time got away and so did their piles of cash. They weren't struggling. Far from it. Still, it had been an easy slide with scads of cash on hand.

"When was it again?"

Why was he pressing the question? Her neck muscles tightened. She breathed in, and her stomach growled. She talked fast to cover for her stomach. "I guess around eight twenty. It was already dark." She hoped her answer distracted from the creaking board, their disintegrating deck, and from her gut grumbling.

"You're hungry." He wasn't looking at her when he commented.

She rolled her eyes.

Typically, Rob had an easy manner. Officially, Jamie found him unsettling.

He glanced up once, then smiled while continuing to focus on the notepad, new words written under the jerky beam of his penlight. "Ya got some loose nails," he said about the deck.

Good lord. Let it go.

"Everything's loose around here, Rob," she said. But as soon as the words slid from her lips, she wished she could suck them back like a duck swallowing a water bug.

Did it sound to him like it sounded to her—that she was loose, too?

"Ya know, I'm a pretty darned good handyman..." he let his words trail away. The suggestion a tricycle handlebar streamer waffling in a breeze.

"We have someone once in a while." The streamer went limp.

He was still writing something...*Is he making a shopping list?* Jamie's attention locked onto his right hand. As his pen bounced across a narrow pocket-sized sheet of paper, he was holding his hand stiff. Then she saw why. It was his right middle knuckle. He had it covered in a bulky, skin-colored bandage, one she hadn't initially spotted. He held the finger slightly elevated, hovering over the others as if it stung him to use it.

"Your finger," she said.

Why did I say anything?

She covered her mouth.

He looked at his finger as if noticing it for the first time, then waved it off. "'S'nothing. Breaking up a fight with an old drunk."

Did he just wince? And if so, because of the memory? Or because of how harsh his words sounded?

He continued his questioning:

"You said you were at a meeting? The book club?"

Why were these questions irking her so much? She brushed it off to their redundancy.

You're not going to catch me in a lie.

She snugged the blue cardigan tighter around her chest.

A wave crashed out somewhere near False Bay, west of where they stood, rolling heavy onto land, its weight pawing at a sandy shoal on the abutting strip of DNR land. As if on cue, a foghorn mewled out east, warning a ferry's sad approach into the marina, into town. The two sounds reminding, *Hey, you live on a rock in the middle of water*. The remoteness and danger of their islet lurked all around.

A rushing vertigo fell over her. She clenched her eyes, swearing to control her balance while dogpaddling through the dizzying wave. Stumbling was not an option. She didn't want Rob to think she was drunk.

"That right?" he asked again. "The book club meeting?"

"Right." She reached toward the wall. Hadn't she mentioned the meeting already?

"You okay?"

"At the library," she said. Heat rose and pooled around her neck like a too tight muffler. "Fine. I'm fine."

"You don't look fine."

"I'm *fine*."

"Okay...did you guys feel the quake?" His eyes brightened like it was the coolest thing, that quake.

Jamie frowned but nodded. "Happened a few hours before the meeting."

"I meant you and Larry," he said.

"Oh." She shivered again. "Yes. We felt it." The dizziness made her queasy. Her hand rose to touch under her nose, but feeling the cool fingerprint on her skin, she decided to place her entire hand over her mouth, then her cheek, her forehead. When she spoke, she gripped both hands together.

"I shouldn't say this, but I love earthquakes," he confessed.

What the hell is wrong with you?

"The lights flickered. Almost went out. The house rolled."

"It was a biggy." He chuckled and kept his eyes locked on hers. "Get the gas turned off?"

"Uh huh."

That's right. No expounding. Yes or no answers only.

"You ever been in one that big?"

"No." She glanced behind her toward the garage. "We didn't have earthquakes in Phoenix. It was horrible. Aren't you going to look for him?" Her question came out too fast, too abruptly.

"Deputies're outside checkin' the woods and road. The culverts." He pointed with his penlight behind him, out to the winding path past the Madrona, past Fox rock, past the mailbox at the entrance of the driveway to the road. Only then, if she squinted, did she notice other flashlights, their beams zigzagging, swinging back and forth like a geisha's white fan, a siren signaling lost ships, seducing a lacework of Madrona branches trimming the south side of their house. And then, as if aliens were emerging out of some cornfield in a horror movie, one more flashlight appeared, then another—one combing the path leading to the drain field and the other over at her mother's vacant house.

She spooked when a couple raccoons snarled, attacked each other, then retreated. The loser whimpered off under some fallen tree trunk for cover. She hadn't yet put out their kibbles. They were hungry.

Rob commented, "Raccoon and people. Funny thing, people'll crawl into a culvert like a raccoon. Lookin' for shelter. Like they're crawling back into the womb." Their eyes connected in what seemed like an accident. She turned away. Her white SUV grayed under the night sky.

"Search & Rescue team's on the way," he said. "Set these guys off lookin' before I knocked. We felt it all the way into town."

"I'm sorry?" she said, then realized he meant the earthquake. "Oh. Yeah. It was big."

"6.7. Knocked out power in town. Here too?"

"No. Amazingly," she said.

The fanning search lights spraying through evergreens gave Jamie the impression of being at a rock concert.

"Thought about coming out to check on you two, what with Larry's condition and all," he said.

Her heart thumped hard. She tried to breathe the maddening patter away. Was she swaying? Maybe she had an inner ear infection.

"You okay?"

She nodded.

"You sure?"

"Larry..." she wanted to cry.

Rimmler glared and locked onto her mouth, then her nose, then each cheek, her eyes finally settling his gaze upon her forehead. Her fingers fluttered up in a dance with his gaze leading her by the hand where to move, finally landing on the edges of her hairline above her eyebrows. She flattened the short stack of bangs, still feeling off-balance. Like teetering at the top of the stairs where she and Larry had argued earlier, right before the quake. Right before everything blurred.

She grabbed for the arm of the deck chair to steady herself.

"You're not okay," he said.

"A little dizzy, I guess. I'm okay. Was that a tremor?" she asked, her fingers bent into a strand of the chair's plastic rattan.

"I didn't feel anything," Rob said. He smiled to the point she thought he might chuckle.

"How embarrassing."

"Not pregnant, are ya?" He smiled.

Is that supposed to be funny?

"Wouldn't that be the worst possible nightmare..." then she added, "...well, other than *this*," meaning Larry.

A single moth spun circles near one of their two porchlights at the door, behind Rob's head, and near the open weave of a spider web. Her body temperature sparked. She pinched at her sweater and fanned herself. First cold. Then hot. Then dizzy. Repeat. Cold. Hot. Dizzy.

When will it all stop?

The moth flitted in circles, orbiting, orbiting its dusty wings attached to its dusty moth body ever closer to the web. She tensed as she watched the beast getting stupidly closer, closer.

When we die, God, do we become like moths, flying stupidly, ever stupidly toward your light, stupidly flying to our end?

Was Larry now some great huge invisible moth soaring in big stupid circles up toward Heaven? Was God a big porchlight in the sky? Where was He now when she needed Him most?

Her body fought the urge to walk over and whisk the bug away to safety because, come on, what would that look like? Rob might think she wasn't amply upset about her missing husband and somehow more concerned about the life of a soon-to-be-dead moth. *Too easily distracted from the topic at hand*, he'd write on his stupid notepad. Because he was there at that very moment because of her missing husband! People have appeared guilty for lesser reasons than being overly concerned about the near death of a moth. So, she tried to ignore the insect and looked out toward the men in the woods.

From her peripheral, Rob was examining her. When she faced him, he squinted high above her brow line. Again, she touched her bangs.

She wished now more than ever that she hadn't cut them herself. But with the COVID thing and all...

"I cut them myself."

Focus.

"I like it. The look." He wrote again on his pad. His fat finger jumping, the odd man out.

Heat flooded Jamie's cheeks and she glanced down at their squeaky deck. Was this an investigation tactic? His eyes observing her, piercing as a rusty nail and a shade of green no kid would ever find in a crayon box, watching for a lie. In his spider web. That's what these guys do, right?

These guys?

But didn't Jamie know Rob? He was, at the very least, a *sort-of* friend. He was always around when she was in town. They always waved to one another. But that's the way it was in Friday Harbor. Where most everyone *sort of* knows everyone else. We're all *sort-of* friends on the rock, a spot one-tenth the size of the largest charted supermall in the US. Jamie knew. She checked once on *Wikipedia*. The mall was somewhere out east, Bloomington, Delaware, or maybe Connecticut. Was there a Bloomington in Connecticut?

Even so…amen.

She tried not to look near the porchlight.

"You in there?" Rob asked.

"Yeah." The word came out measly. Breathy.

She knew what he was thinking. What they *all* were thinking. Those ones out there with their sodium sparks making a light show all the way to the top of the trees.

Did they really think Larry had climbed a tree?

It's usually the spouse who kills the other spouse in these situations.

Isn't that true? That's what Liv always says about storytelling. "You can angle away from the spouse as much as you want, throw in a red herring here and there, but in the end, the spouse is, nine times out of ten, guilty." And she would know. Wasn't she a famous *NY Times* bestseller who made her living writing crime novels and thrillers? She'd interviewed dozens of lawyers and detectives about this sort of thing. She'd gotten her training on the job and was well-versed in legalese as well as legal goings-on.

At first, the fame drew Jamie to Liv and later her personality and caring nature. Plus, when you first met her, you would never know she was a knife-wielding woman. She'd learned knife throwing while writing of one of her bestsellers. That book got optioned then made into a film. She figured the knife brought her luck.

Anyway, she never left the house without a seven-inch blade, a fixed throwing knife. Said it made her feel safe. She kept it strapped in an ankle holster. She even wore the damn thing with dresses.

Liv was fun that way. Different. Challenging. Jamie felt they were cohorts in crime, and they became best friends.

Jamie's heart thumped hard again. Just once this time like a grandfather clock striking a shift from lunchtime to one. Yes. She was hungry. How could she be hungry at a time like this? At once, she felt guilty. To eat or not to eat. Was that the question? What about a hunger strike? A hunger strike sounds an apt punishment.

You mustn't lose your people.

She placed her hand just below her breasts but drew Rob's attention. So, she slipped her hand fully around her waist and swiped a quick hand across her bangs, glanced down at her feet hoping to divert Rob's eyes away from her chest, and turned away, again glancing at anything behind her, past the red, metal garage toward the darkened woods edging the property of the neighbors, Rick and Taylor. She wondered if they'd heard her earlier, if they'd heard her crying for Larry. She wondered if Rick had his drone up now after noticing police lights flashing. Or if he'd had them up at all today. Was he taking photos?

Breathe. Will they find Larry?

Just breathe.

She tried to smile. Her cheek muscles twitched. Her teeth bared. Was *that* a smile? Or was it instead the grimace by some evil carnival clown?

The moth had disappeared. Had the spider snagged it?

No, she thought, at first.

But then she saw. A witness to the aftermath of a crime. Its dusty wings must have brushed a strand of silk igniting the spider into action. The predator, unleashed onto its rope bridge, darting straight for its struggling prey.

Was the spider female? And were all female spiders like black widows—killers of their mates? She closed her eyes and took in a deep breath.

Breathe it away.

Isn't that how she used to do it?

Wipe the memory clean.

Like when she was a kid and something bad happened. She was so clever at it back then, wiping bad memories away.

Behind the garage, tree frogs were singing in an ad hoc choir, making the woods that banked her property ring like the piccolo section of the Tabernacle Choir. The waxy salal and white trident shaped *Holodiscus discolor*, commonly named *ocean spray*, were the frogs' audience, swaying and cheering in the night breeze. Did the frogs sing for the success of the spider? Or for the death of the moth?

Something slapped the surface of the duck pond. Afterwards, the quacking began. Mallards burst into the air. Probably a fox gunning for one of the ducks. Then more splashing and quacking and then silence. No bursting into air. Just the deathly void of sound.

"Will they search the ponds?" she said. Anyone walking blind might take a header into one of the black ponds surrounding their property.

"Search & Rescue has gear for that."

She nodded and dragged her eyes away from his. And she hoped to God he wouldn't ask the question she dreaded most...

...the one they always do on the cop shows...

...the question if Larry and she were getting along...

...about the sudden sparks and bouts of venom flying between them. Those infrequent, sporadic fits. An epileptic body twisting out of its own control. The cursing. Finding momentary solitude separated in a room.

To any safe room. Shut the door. Lock it.

Put distance between the boxers. To your corners!

Find a safe place to wallow in anger then penance, the shift from penance to an overwhelming pity, and finally to the fights ending the usual way, in face-to-face apologies. Apologies made by Jamie to Larry because, by the time she calmed down, the dementia had wiped clean Larry's memory of the fights.

There was a poem circling the internet once by Unknown about how you're not supposed to yell at someone with dementia. She needed that wisdom so much that she taped the poem on the door of the refrigerator.

One of the stanzas said,

Don't lose your patience with me.

Do not scold or curse or cry.

I can't help the way I'm acting.

Can't be different 'though I try.

Jamie took it to mean: They don't understand what's happening.

Don't yell. Just smile.

Try to smile.

And right then and there, she wanted to be Unknown.

However, their fight today blew a cannonball through the poem. She didn't control her anger like the poem instructed.

The fight ended badly, not in their typical apology. It just stopped dead. Fell into oblivion and shattered on the ground. And now Larry was gone.

A missing spouse, Rob spoke into his shoulder radio. Why not missing person? Why make the distinction of spouse? Because Liv was right. That's why. Authorities always suspected the surviving spouse in cases where the other had died.

As if all these thoughts had taken form and appeared overhead in some morbid kind of quote bubble, etched in fat white letters against the night's black background, Rimmler, keeping his eyes locked on his notepad (intentionally locked, it seemed to Jamie), he asked, "You two getting along okay these days?"

CHAPTER 2
NOW—September 21, 2020

I'm suffocating. A thick woolen blanket stuffed inside my lungs.

Look, I'm not an arms-length acter in this whole issue. Not distant enough from the problem, let alone clear-headed about this matter, to give it a universal spin. My heart beats every second about this problem, about my husband, about our last day spent together.

Jamie Michaels is *not* my husband's name. It's *mine*. He's Larry. Or was.

I had thrown, as I do until I have time, all my paperwork into the inbox for later dissemination and filing. To say my inbox was full is akin to saying that the hippopotamus over *there* will fit into this golf cart over *here*. Enough said, the inbox was *over*full.

But back to my point. A person needs to understand how extremely upsetting it is to hear that a foot, which washed up on the shores of your own island, might be the right foot of your husband. *Upsetting*, for a myriad of reasons, as one might suspect, but mostly because both his feet were fully attached to him the last time I saw Larry alive.

The by-product of the article was that it all became real. Up until now, everything felt dreamy. It wasn't really happening. I'd been floating through this abstract fantasy, this horror, but now, like a slap across the face, the article snapped me into the present.

It's not that I didn't expect Larry to be the one to die first. Most women believe they will outlive their husbands. For no other reason but for mere demographic stats.

I'm twenty-one years Larry's junior. People here had a heyday talking about our age difference when we began dating. They got over it after some better gossip circulated through the island grapevine. People either didn't care about the gap in our ages or else they distanced themselves from us or out-and-out told us how wrong it was, using the haggard example of, "When he was twenty-five, you were four!" But as a forty-something adult, I had every right to marry whoever I wanted. But people who hate things like this don't hear you and fall back on the child-adult-pedophilia example...*every single time.*

I called the authorities about Larry going missing a month after our twelfth anniversary.

People still say "missing" so they don't have to say "died." When *Larry went missing* is far more hopeful than when Larry *died.*

He had dementia and the house was getting away from us. But for ten great years, Larry was a vibrant, physical, rational man who loved golfing, riding his bike, and taking walks with me. He was tall, not lean but not heavy, he had the bluest eyes I've ever seen. I could drown in those eyes, and his hair was a shock of white that he kept trimmed à la businessman cut once a month at his favorite barber by the beef jerky shop. I think that barber was his favorite *because* of the beef jerky shop. He always returned sharp and smelling salty with his lips tasting of leather.

His favorite color was red. But he wasn't wearing red that last day. I had dressed him—had been dressing him for about six months.

We hadn't seen the kids, Larry's kids, since the summer of 2019. It had always been a hassle between family members getting together, what with us living on a remote island and everyone else a simple road trip away from one another. A couple months without seeing family in Washington was normal for us but when COVID hit, we became acutely aware of the extended time separated from our loved ones. Well, Larry's loved ones. And it was more that I became aware because Larry, by then, had started to forget their names. All my family still lived in Phoenix where I grew up. As a middle-aged woman who moved away, I was used to not seeing family for long stretches in between visits.

Larry's kids, Dennis and Michelle, haven't called in months, not since Larry's disappearance. They all but told me that they both thought I'd done something. That his disappearance was my fault. What do you do with that? What do you say?

For a while, we both worked. He at his convenience store in town. Me at insurance investigations—claims, fraud and whatnot. After work, we would set off maintaining a home the way anyone with five acres and a three-thousand-square-foot home manages.

Once a month, my book club friends would meet at our house. It was logistically best for everyone, and they enjoyed our nine-foot-long pine table in the living room. That it was situated near the fireplace didn't hurt either. But we stopped meeting at our home because I couldn't keep up with the house, what with taking care of Larry. We ended up moving the meetings to the library.

My girlfriend, and dare I say *best* friend, Liv, was concerned. She offered to have Paul come over with her and help us around the house. I couldn't ask that of someone. Everyone is busy. I refused. Pride has a funny way of making us think we can manage when, clearly, we cannot.

Still, she persisted in asking to help us. And still, I refused her kind offers. After Larry stopped working, I stepped into his shoes at the convenience store. For a while I tried to manage both my insurance investigations and claims but had to cut back on the hours. Fortunately, we had two managers—one for days and one for nights—who could run the store blindfolded. So, when it got to the point that I couldn't leave Larry alone anymore, they stepped in full-hearted, only needing me for things only a corporate officer could handle. The store did and does well. We had eleven employees including me and Larry, plus we had a nice retirement plan that we didn't want to touch until we had to.

Before Larry got too bad, once a week on Fridays, Benito, our landscaper, worked magic around the grounds with his weed-whacker, clearing off clippings and leaves with his blower, giving us time to straighten the inside after our workday had ended, to fix dinner, drink a glass of wine, and settle into the evening relaxing from our nine-to-fives.

But on weekends and sometimes after work during weeks of nicer weather, Larry pressure-washed mold that had covered paint on the lower part of the house. I cleaned higher, like carving out all the muck that collected in our gutters. That had to be my job. Larry was afraid of heights. And I was too but I guess not as much as Larry, who would freeze at the slightest sense of falling. That's the fear with heights. In extreme cases, with some people standing on flat ground, if they're too high up but can see the ground below, their heads spin, they get dizzy, and feel like they're about to fall.

Even so, I often worried about falling—that if I fell if I would die instantly or languish miserably on the ground, my brains spilled out on a rock, my back broken waiting for death before actually dying, being aware that I would succumb with death's grip pulling me under.

Morbid scenes played out in different ways each time I went up to clean off the shingles.

I slip on a patch of moss and lose my balance.

I stub my toe, trip, and off I'd go, ass over teakettle.

Murder bees attack and force me to my death.

Each cleaning brought forth a new death scenario.

So, to prevent any mishaps, I dressed appropriately. I would slip on a headband and pull my hair back in a scrunchy to keep my hair out of my face, and wore tighter fitting pants, like leggings, for less chance of snagging on something or getting tangled around my shoes and causing me to fall.

Over the years, the whole process became tried and true. I would jerry-rig two tethers complete with carabiners and rope, fastening each clip to a thick belt with two ropes—one tied off onto a tree in the backyard to secure me while I worked on the front yard side of the roof, and another tied to a front yard tree while I worked on the backyard side of the roof. There were several lead vent pipes sticking out of the composite tile roof making it easy for tripping. The double ropes were heavy and cumbersome but necessary. After securing myself, I got to work removing moss off the shingles with a landscape scraper. Next, I used a heavy stiff brush to reef out the cracks from every inch of our tiles, and after that I used a blower to remove from two hundred feet of aluminum gutters all that had collected over the previous twelve months, like fir needles, Madrona leaves, and a myriad of other refuse disposed of by the earth. Thank God it was only a once-a-year task.

Home maintenance and projects were sort of our *thing*, for lack of a better word—to manicure fascia and ductwork that edged the eaves on the upper *and* lower roofline. I was actually good at it too. With the tether, I was safe, and I enjoyed being alone up on the roof and often sang an old song by James Taylor about the experience of looking high over a place, viewing it from a spot no one else might ever see…"Up on the Roof." A place of peace and quiet.

We also did more mundane things as well, like raking decaying leaves into piles that we wheelbarrowed behind a huge Douglas fir where we kept compost. The compost area had three stations, one for new leaves, one for leaves in partial decay, and a third for fully composted material, the stuff we used for landscaping jobs.

We swept the porches and decks, trimmed the boxwood and

barberry hedges, and pruned the maple trees in the center of our driveway. Turning the compost from one station into the next as was necessary. Those were my jobs, mostly.

Larry's main job was to jump on the riding mower and take down the grass of several acres between the mother-in-law house, the front yard, and the back field all the way down to the pond.

We hired people for more difficult or skilled jobs like cutting in a new door where there had once been only a window or building a separate garage where there had once been an old shed in the shape of a small barn.

But we weren't special in our maintenance jobs. Everyone on the island was busy futzing around their homes, maintaining them. Until, of course, we couldn't. Well, until Larry couldn't.

It happened slowly. Problems began to arise. Things began breaking down.

The riding mower began to fail *often*, or so Larry said. "The battery's dead."

"Again?" I'd say.

We called Stan out to charge it. Once it roared to life again, Larry could plow down the grass, and after two hours he'd come in. But that stopped too. His mowing began to worsen. The ground, from the mother-in-law house all the way to the pond, looked patchy and strange, mazelike, a series of lines cut in between high and low grass, sometimes crisscrossing, sometimes up and back exhibiting a pattern of green earth, large swaths Larry missed entirely, appearing like a *Gulliver's Travels* game for enormous mice.

Too often, he buried the mower, sinking it deep into wet earth in areas he'd miscalculated for safe maneuvering. What I didn't realize is that these were signs of cognitive malfunction. I didn't realize it back, then with everything hindsight allows, the past comes into stark focus. What had been strange and fuzzy became clear and horrifying. My husband's brain was eroding like someone taking an etch-a-sketch to it and making thin lines thick and dull and wide.

We would hear Benito drive in with his gurgling Toyota truck. The thing had to be twenty years old. Larry went out to greet him. That's how it normally happened.

One day, however, after Benito drove in, I heard his truck gurgle around the circular drive and back out onto the street, then leave.

Larry burst back through the door, slamming it behind him, his face glowing with anger.

I hovered over all fourteen steps on the landing. He stood at the bottom of the stairs near the front door. I was multitasking with a toothbrush in my mouth and pulling my hair into a rubber band at the same time. I intended to clean out old seed, straw, and bird droppings from inside our three aviaries where we kept our ringed-neck doves. I wanted to do it while Benito was here so that he could help me move what I would be gutting out of the aviaries. Benito could take them to the compost pile.

"Did he leave?" I said about Benito, my mouth full of paste and brush.

"I fired him," Larry said.

"*What*? Why?" A glob of toothpaste jettisoned and landed on the stair below the landing where I stood. My hair pulled back by then tight enough to take the wrinkles from the crow's feet around my eyes.

"I didn't like what he was doing."

"Like what?" I pressed.

"He was lazy."

"He helped us a lot, Larry."

"We don't need him. I can do everything he does."

I brushed at my teeth a little, then, after a second, I said, "It *will* save us some money." My words foamy and white.

"Right." His face darkened. He rubbed his right hand over his head, took great interest in his shoes, then situated his feet in what I used to know as ballet's first position. It was a thing that became common months later, first position. Finding any corner in the house and situating his feet in the exact ninety-degree angle, like the corner of a rug or a plank in the wood floor.

So, when he fired Benito, we let it go because I figured between the two of us, we could manage. How wrong could I have been? Back then, I didn't realize Larry had fully entered stage one of dementia, that dementia had already begun searing its acid torch into Larry's brain.

Within one year, none of our lawnmowers worked. We had three. Nary a one functioned. At least, Larry couldn't get them to run. The blowing off of leaves and dirt that Benito used to do wasn't getting done either, because now the *blower* was broken. And after the blower, the weed-whacker.

Within two years, the grass had grown hip high. Mold took over the northside paint on the house. The gutters became...well, what I called the "second-story garden." Seeds had filled and established growth into small wispy alders bending their thin shoots with every wafting breeze that came along. Grassy plants wrapped a furry edge all the way around the roof. The moss sandwiched between making mossy loaves on every tile of the upper and lower roofs. The musty scent filled the air every time the wind blew. We were living in a house maintenance nightmare.

I guess it would be redundant to say that things got away from me. Mighty redundant. But they got away from Larry too and not just maintenance projects. His brain had gone AWOL. He could do little more than mutter around the house, sit in front of the TV, and eat when I brought him food. We stopped taking walks together; I never knew if he might mess his clothes.

So, not only did chores get away from him, but so did his physical activity. We weren't taking our usual walks down our street. That's when I took up running. I would get up an hour or two before Larry woke up to take off on a run. At first the runs were short, only halfway down the road, about a third of a mile. After a while I was running a mile, then two, and then I could make the full circle from our front door, west on our road past False Bay, down the long road of the horse ranch, out to Bailer Hill, up to Little Road, out to Cattle Point Road, and back to False Bay Road to our doorstep—a full 6.2 miles in a matter of just over an hour. And I needed to stay fit, as it turned out, to help Larry when he fell out of bed or got stuck on the floor in the bathroom or when he couldn't figure out how to get out of the back of the truck off the tailgate. I needed physical strength. And I had it.

Soon, he was making other mistakes like with his medicine, medicine that if you *do* make mistakes, it can kill you. I took over administering and setting up his weekly A.M.-P.M. pill box. A.M. is purple and P.M. is blue.

He already needed diapers, but we waited because it embarrassed him. After we got those, we called them briefs because the packaging labeled them as "protective" briefs. Briefs was less embarrassing to Larry.

Next, he needed my help getting in and out of bed, up from his chair, off the toilet.

And so now, here we are, up to date, with a foot getting away from someone. Possibly Larry's foot. Probably. Why else would Rob Rimmler call me? Why would he alert me about the newspaper article? Not unless he knew. Right?

By the way, why do feet always wash ashore? It seems far more feet than any other body parts—an oddity, me-thinks—wash up onto land. Is it some abstract form of final selection? Like, aha! You can take my life, but you can't take my feet!

As I scrolled back and forth through each line of the article, sometimes gazing out the window—once maybe twice—it seemed we were running headlong into a bit of nasty weather. A violence of clouds painted the sky—a violence not lost on me as I sit and read the online local paper. With clouds so dense and the sun—a razzmatazz red dot of crayon color setting its spark outside the lines of the sky, a blush of clouds farther north, near the tip of the island. The clouds scudding by, end over end, for me boded *trouble a-brewing*—a term I picked up from watching old Westerns and spending half my life in the hot sandy landscape of Phoenix.

And, at once, a one-hundred-ten boiling fever set a flame out of my hypothalamus gland at the thought of that city. That's what post-menopause is like. Just the thought of heat and you're hot. One second your body temp regulator says, *Hey, everything here's just peachy keen!* The next second, your body temp regulator spring goes *Twoing*! And your heat? Haywire.

And as I sat considering the sky, the weather, I realized how similar clouds had rolled in the day Larry picked that fight with me. The day of the earthquake. Yes, that same day he went missing, three months ago, June 20, 2020. His birthday, for God's sake...on his *birthday*.

But he didn't remember it was his birthday. Larry didn't remember much. Just things from long ago. The week before, he thought it was November and got all excited about Thanksgiving dinner. He wanted me to make a turkey with all the fixins—mashed potatoes and gravy, sweet potatoes, green beans. I mean, I *made* it for him because, why not? But Thanksgiving loomed several months off, and a turkey in June is a heck of a lot more expensive at the local market than one nearer Thanksgiving holiday.

I used to wallow in a pigsty of denial about Larry's dementia. I made excuses his decline was a mix of prescription drugs. But after bagging the bulk of those drugs, I researched online for any concerning side effects between the only two remaining and finding none, I decided to take Larry to his cardiologist, Dr. Nickel, like the coin. I explained what was going on because, of course because Larry couldn't explain for himself, and asked if Dr. Nickel knew of any other just-as-effective blood pressure meds out there that didn't cause his runny nose or the gurgling congestion he was now suffering from. The frustration I felt, and how Larry must have felt, was all part of Larry not being able to express himself.

So many physical and mental failings, things that began slow, were now avalanching at breakneck speed and sweeping away my sweet husband in the wake. And when he forgot what month it was, well, the mud in the pigsty dried up. I couldn't deny any longer. I called Gigi and said, "I'm not in denial anymore." She made a sad sound and let me talk. I told her how I wouldn't fool myself into thinking his dementia was going to get better.

Again, Gigi made another sad sound, then again said, "I know." And what was behind that I know was a community *we know* and possibly *we've all known all along and you're the only one on the planet who is stupid enough to not know.*

It was nothing Gigi ever experienced—to care for an ailing husband or child or parent, for that matter. And that was the turning point. When I shifted my role from deeply concerned wife to deeply concerned caregiver. I remember praying about it and emerging from one morning prayer meditation aware and bright with insight that Larry was Larry just not the same as when we first dated eighteen years before or when we married seventeen years before or, hell, even three years ago. He was Larry but now Larry with dementia.

Married for eighteen years! A nano-fraction on the yardstick of eternity. A microsecond in the winds created off the drag of our planet as it hurtles through space and time. Barely an atom in a baby's breath.

Larry had moved in a couple years after I bought my place, a country home on a five-acre plot. Five acres, mostly wooded and uninhabitable with the acreage split in half by a long, wide crevice of rocks ranging from man-size to boulders all edging the crack scarring the earth torn and jagged as if when the earth rent away it opened its mouth and heaved from its belly a vomit of earth and boulders.

The previous owners had crisscrossed several boards over the gap then topped it off with the a few pieces of inch-thick plywood to prevent animals from falling in, he'd said. He'd also said he did it because of his daughter. She *made* him do it. After buying the land ten years before and after a day spent exploring the land with the girl, she made the previous owner promise, "Daddy, promise me! Please." She begged him.

He'd said, "She was so upset about animals, mostly deer falling in." He also said that the crevice had been there since ancient times, but the daughter was so unnerved by the width and depth of the crevice that he knelt to her wishes.

And I wondered how he knew about the age of the crevice but forgot to ask about that point. I was swept away by the story of his daughter. After, he led me off to other parts of the land he was hoping to sell me. He talked about things we didn't have in Phoenix. Things like the septic tanks and the septic drain field. Those sat back on the other side of the crevice. We needed to drive to get to them. On our walk around the land, pink surveyor flags appeared every few yards. The flags demarcated the lot boundary line from the neighbor's.

At the end of our back field, sat a ten-acre pond with opalescent winged mallards that burst into flight when we approached.

And, I assumed association with the ducks when he said, "And a fox. We have fox too. One we call 'Foxy. she's a resident here, has had several litters of kits—cute as the dickens."

And I almost didn't buy the place. With the crevice boarded up like that, well, it made an impression on me. Let's just say to me it was like sacred ground, that if the daughter was correct, many hundreds, if not thousands, of animals' carcasses, bones, and remains, maybe even human, were already forming fossils in whatever material lay at the bottom—another point the owner made...how no one had ever been able to tap the bottom. A severe wave of the heebie-jeebies coursed over my skin, raising hair like little military men standing at attention. He'd said that no matter how long a shaft they used...and let his words drift down to the depths of the crevice.

"How long?" I pressed. I needed to know. It sort of freaked me out.

"They got the well guy out. He could only go down six hundred feet."

"Good God," I said, and touched the gold crucifix around my neck.

By ten years and the daughter long gone, gaps had grown between the crevice and his makeshift covering. What if an animal, a deer or my *cat,* fell in or got stuck struggling, thrashing between boards, squealing for their lives? The thought tormented me. That's when I decided to keep the cat in. Back then the cat was Winky. Winky had been a city cat and not well-equipped to live in the country anyway, so in she stayed. I mean, what if she or any animal, for that matter, got a leg caught? Had to chew it or wrench it off as they struggled to break free to save their lives?

Which brings me back to the lost and now found human foot. Was it Larry's? It had to be.

It was obvious from the article that authorities hadn't yet abandoned Larry's investigation. In fact, it appeared it was very much heating up.

My Larry was part of the news cycle. He was possibly "a man's foot." All that's left. But you have to understand, there was so much more to Larry than what they found washed up on South Beach. He was a gentle, genteel elderly man with all appendages attached last time we chatted. Yes, before the book club meeting at the library. Except for his sudden and rare bouts of confusion and anger. The Larry I knew was charming and funny. He loved to laugh. He loved for me to tickle him. He loved his tee shirt that said: *IF YOU TICKLE ME, I'M NOT RESPONSIBLE FOR YOUR INJURIES.* A tee shirt that made me tickle him even more for no other reason but the dare. And I *bought* him the shirt!

Am I still holding out hope for my Larry? Holding out hope for something known to be impossible? Isn't that some obscure definition of insanity? No. I know for a fact he's dead. And I will not let my mind sink into some quicksand of misplaced hope that he's alive. I know Larry's not alive.

Anyway, when one thinks about it, if the foot *does* belong to Larry, how could he *not* be dead?

Denial has no claim on me. It won't sweep me into fantasy. Larry is dead. For anyone to believe otherwise, well, they're simply kidding themselves. He's long dead. Three months dead. No one can walk away one foot detached and survive.

I hope I don't cry tomorrow. I hate to cry in front of people.

They'd understand. Three months isn't a long time after the loss of one's husband. I mean, Gigi still grieves, and her husband has been dead since 2008. Twelve years seems an awfully long stretch for grieving. Brian's was so sudden—a widow-maker, the doctors had told her. He was alive one second, and boom! The next? Dead.

I suppose Larry's was similarly sudden. In the house one moment in time for the earthquake, before the book club. Then neatly absent the next moment when I came home. Never to be found. Lost somewhere on the island.

Everyone knew. People listened to the deputy radio station.

The news flashed through the island like a heat-seeking missile.

And now, this foot turns up. It's all over Facebook on the "What's Up, Friday Harbor?" page.

The day he went missing repeats and repeats, each crucial second sequenced with little variation in scene setting, dialogue, facial expression, *combustion*.

"You're killing me!" he'd yelled. It was a couple hours before I had to leave for the meeting that day. His statement harkened back to something funny I'd heard before like "You're killing me, Smalls." But Larry wasn't laughing. Larry was exhibiting full-on, out-and-out fury.

I was putting out some food for him. Snacks and drinks enough from then until I returned from our book club's monthly meeting. I'd left him alone before. He'd never gone missing before. Never ventured out. Was happy to putter to the kitchen and back with snacks and drinks.

But this night when I returned and they showed up to help, well, it reminded me of so many news reports about old men in Bellingham or Burlington, in Seattle—ending up lost and never to be found. Because on the mainland, there's room to wander.

But our island? Where we live a captive audience by the island's surrounding water? No. If you go missing here, chances are pretty high someone will find you.

So, when he screamed at me that I was going to kill him? Kill my Larry? Good lord. Well, I didn't mean to glance away. I honestly can't remember if I rolled my eyes but must have. Probably did. Yes, I did. I take full responsibility because what else would have sparked such outrage?

He fumed.

I tried to explain.

I scanned the counter for his medicine. He needed a citalopram tablet. I didn't like giving them to him regularly because of the numbing effect. But for times like this? Hell, yeah. The citalopram was an anti-anxiety-anti-depressant winning combination that worked like a gem—a saying from Dad when he was alive. "That worked like a gem, Jamie," he'd say. That saying always made me laugh even when I knew he was about to say it. He got this look. His *tell*. He was so funny.

But I'd been rushing around, getting ready to leave for the meeting and had little patience that day, I admit. And even though it was a couple hours before, I needed to get a few things done around the house—Lester's cat box, another load of Larry's soiled laundry. I figured I could squeeze in a bit of weed-whacking. The edges of the garden around the front steps up to the porch were looking weedy and dry. It was a good day too. I had a few minutes I could squeeze it in. Time was something I had been short on since segueing into this new lifestyle with Larry.

I have time. That's the sort of thing we tell ourselves. That we have time.

I needed him to take his pill and have some snacks, needed to add two items to my notes on the book we were discussing that night—a great story called *The Gretchen Question* by Jessica Treadway—her throwaway sentences that were not throwaway at all but metaphorical and landmarks within the story.

And I still needed to take a shower and fix my hair. Screw makeup. I didn't have time for that. Lipstick would be enough.

Instead, here's Larry affronting me, saying that I was trying to *kill* him.

"What are you talking about?" How could he think I wanted to kill him? All I did was *care* for him. But before I could contain it, my anger bubbled. It flashed. Suddenly, like Larry's.

Thinking back, I should've known. Asking questions like, *What are you talking about?* to someone with an addled brain about what or why he was thinking this or that might easily plunk the questioner into the pool of dementia alongside the demented.

He barreled up at me, away from where he was standing at my desk, and brandished a printout in my face—an article I had downloaded for a client who used to live on Orcas Island but who had moved north to Bellingham. The article was in reference to life insurance policies on missing persons. He'd found my research for a *client* thinking it was about him. Then he shoved the papers into my chest and knocked me back a step.

But when I gathered the papers, our hands brushed against each other's. His were icy. Mine were hot.

My anger sat its ass down and my caregiver stepped up. "Are you cold?"

"Don't act like you give a damn about me! *Me*! Your husband. Remember? The one you're trying to kill!"

During previous bouts of psychoses, Larry had never once become this violent. I mean, of course I'd read about wives of dementia patients waking up with their husband's hands around their necks and fighting for their lives—a sign of dementia escalating. This had to be that.

After studying reams and reams of online information, I came across one that referred to seven distinct phases of dementia and its progress. With phase one--the sneakiest phase and most insidious phase—there are no warning signs of any problems. Everything seems hunky-dory in phase one of dementia.

In phase two, however, a person experiences an awareness, a sense that something feels different and might be wrong. They question their own mental stability in this phase which usually goes undiagnosed because they or, like in Larry's case, their loved ones, think they're being silly. Worrying about nothing. Denial in others is a key factor why treatment doesn't begin sooner. It's the family's hesitation to believe the patient has dementia.

With phase three, people around the patient begin to notice deficits in the person's ability to perform demanding job situations. Difficulties concentrating on tasks at hand. Often getting sidetracked and unable to command a single thought. They're still conversational in phase three but they bounce around, ping-pong, if you will, between several topics sometimes during a single conversation.

In phase four, people require assistance performing complicated tasks such as handling finances and traveling. And this is key—I found real problems with our finances when I took over managing the bills and our money. We were headed backwards, not forward on our home equity line of credit. He'd been tapping into the HELOC regularly without me knowing. And with our short trip back to Phoenix for only three nights, Larry had an accident in the Everett terminal. He couldn't keep his pants up as he walked. The pantlegs dragged under his shoes with him holding his belt to prevent them from falling off completely. An extra difficult task with him rolling luggage behind him, luggage that kept squirreling out of control and often tipping over. Something I kept yelling at him about because, as I screamed, "we're going to be late." Standing fifty feet ahead of him, yelling. Who does that? Then, finally, doubling-up my own luggage onto his and holding up his pants in the back so they wouldn't fall off all the while wheeling our carry-ons into the terminal and up to a sharp-suited flight attendant at the desk.

Hindsight offers clarity and wisdom for the future. It also offers up a whole bagful of guilt.

During phase five, a person begins a decline to the point he requires assistance choosing clothing. They often appear wearing clothing they had on several previous days which, if unchecked, could go on for weeks. That had become commonplace with Larry. All these things occurred within three years of Larry's first suspicions that something was going wrong with his brain.

Of course, I wouldn't dare allow Larry to go weeks in the same outfit, the same socks, and probably briefs for more than a few days. I took up my caregiving mantel in small bites and began laying out new socks, new underpants, new shirts, and trousers while he took a shower and removing the worn clothing to the laundry hamper.

Phase six shows a more drastic decline. The patient needs assistance the way a child might need assistance. Like with bathing and going to the bathroom (or "toileting" as the article read). During phase six, the patient might experience urinary and fecal incontinence. That's where Larry had been for a quite a while when he went missing.

But the final phase, phase seven, is the cruelest of all other phases. It's the phase when a patient loses his ability to speak, his vocabulary declining to fewer than twelve intelligible words. In this final, seventh phase, he will also lose the ability to walk, sit up, smile, or hold up his head.

I used to keep the article under my notebook—a journal I scribbled into now and again. You know, thoughts of the day, some poetry, ideas, Larry's progression into this slow terrible death. I kept it in my desk drawer, so I knew how to prepare for things to come. If anyone can prepare for something like that—preparing to keep a vegetable alive. The cruelest of all phases. For the patient and the caregiver because, truly, how can one prepare the witnessing of a human being turning back into a fetus?

I didn't want Larry to suffer through this final stage. If there was a God, and I knew then and know now that there is, He would set out a plan to prevent Larry from having to suffer this last and most horrible of phases. This was my prayer: "Please God, don't let him suffer. Don't let him be scared. Make it fast."

I thought we had more time. A child's whimsy.

We did not.

"Evidence!" he screamed at me. "Evidence you're trying to kill me!"

I need to make clear how angry he was. He was boiling at me.

He must have gone through the files in my inbox. The printout was research for a client whose husband fell overboard off their yacht near Lummi Island but whose body they never recovered and deemed lost at sea, until a few months later when his body washed ashore. The article relayed in gruesome detail how a man's body, partially eaten away by sea creatures, had floated up onto shore near Doe Bay on Orcas. Like he was trying to get home. I envisioned his zombie-like body swimming in a choppy sea taking choppy strokes, fighting off seals and sea lions, kicking at them as his zombie form swam back to his home island.

He'd been missing over six months before the authorities deemed him dead. Then the body showed up. I'd pulled the file again, printed it out to show the research I'd done, and was intending to send it along with a past due notice of her invoice.

So earlier that day, the same day Larry went missing, the day he flipped out on me, I flipped out on him in response. I'd had it. There's only so much a wife can take. I was running my own company, assisting the managers who now were running Larry's store, I was taking care of him and the house. I was ragged and tired and ready for a break. I decided to set up an appointment with Dana—a well-respected caregiver—to help me out with Larry a couple days a week. We decided on a date two weeks later. Two weeks, as it turned out, too late.

In my defense, Larry *knew* he wasn't supposed to go through my work files. As an insurance investigator, some of the information is confidential. Everything—all my frustration, all my exhaustion, all my sadness—bubbled up at once in the form of anger with Larry but also in anger with me. Because I was supposed to be able to keep it together. My mind wasn't the addled, squishy brain as was Larry's. A person should be able to control themselves when dealing with someone in need of care.

Anger flashed between us with him railing at me and me railing back. It was frightening. His screaming, his hulking form on the landing at the top of the stairs, him trying to intimidate me. Him going through my *work*?

I yelled back, knowing you're not supposed to yell at someone with dementia. It confuses them further. Makes them feel inadequate. Their normal flight-or-fight systems broken, they become further flustered, and instead of remaining angry or hurt, they become lost or find all of it funny—forgetting entirely why they are upset or frustrated or why they were yelling in the first place. Their emotional responses get muddy and become a flotsam of memories, a soup, all mixing into each other.

Anger becomes humor. Sadness becomes happy.

But I didn't stop. God help me. "You stupid old man." My lips curled around each word. "You have dementia! You don't even know if you had eggs this morning but you're sure. Oh my God. You're sure I'm trying to *kill* you?!"

It was heartless. As soon as the word flew out of my mouth, I prayed I could take them back. If for no other reason than for telling someone you love that their brain is failing. That information should never be spoken.

My throat tightened and my sight blurred when his expression changed after hearing the word *dementia*. And I prayed again, that his condition would cause him to forget that I told him he had dementia.

CHAPTER 3
THEN—June 20, 2020

"You two having any issues?" Rob had to repeat the question.

Jamie tried to appear nonchalant but not so much that he would doubt anything she said. "You mean, issues like living with someone who has dementia?" But she didn't stop there. "You mean, like caring for them morning, noon, and night, showering them, feeding them, changing their diapers, making sure they take their pills, driving them to the doctor and back, hoping they don't fall down," she took a breath in, then continued, "and then helping them up when they do? You mean, issues like that?" She couldn't, didn't want to control her accusatory tone. "Nah, Rob. We got no issues."

But they always suspect the spouse.

"Check," he said, seemingly forgiving her rude response. Then, "It's a real shame about Larry. Everyone feels bad for yo—" he stopped short and corrected his words, "for him. Ya know, for you both. 'Specially, right after your mom and all. Just seems like a lot."

She pressed her lips together and shook her head. They had no idea. Unless you live through it...no idea.

"I appreciate that, Rob," she said. Then after a pause, added, "It's been tough. To say the least."

"You gonna sell?"

"Sell?"

"The store."

What the hell business is it of yours?

"No. I don't know. I'm not sure. Not yet." Her eyes fluttered. "I need to sit." She backed up but stumbled. Rob caught her by the elbow and helped her to one of the two rattan deck chairs.

He was about to ask her if she was okay, and said, "It were me? I'd…" But he got distracted by one of the two deputies with flashlights. He waved the beam of light in front of him as he walked the curved driveway, the light bouncing with each step like a ball over words of a sing-along song. He didn't get the chance to tell her what *he'd* do if the tables were turned. Like *that* was any of his business either.

"Sarge!" The deputy called.

"Jus a sec, Alec!" With his attention broken, Rob turned back.

"Wait here," he said to Jamie, then, skipped down three rock stairs, and met Alec halfway down the circular driveway. They kept their voices low.

Too low for Jamie to hear clearly but not low enough for her to hear him say *the gorge.*

CHAPTER 4
NOW—September 21, 2020

Can skin really crawl?

I had scrolled down past the article to read people's comments. Some were gross while others were compassionate. One of the grosser ones posited that the body parts might be some serial killer either on or around the island.

When my phone jangled, I nearly jumped out of my skin and dribbled coffee onto a few keys of my laptop, which I still had open to the article. A morphing pool of beige spread ever near my phone. Without thinking, I inadvertently set the mug right back down into the spill and began fumbling, choosing between saving the laptop or saving the phone. The laptop won. The phone got a little wet but nothing my sweatpants couldn't absorb.

It was Afon. He was probably checking on me again. With all his bad points, and believe me Afon had plenty, he was still kind to check on me. Still, I didn't want to speak with him. I didn't want to be bothered. He'd already called. When is it okay to tell someone that they're bothering you? Is it ever? I couldn't contain my attitude. Nor did I want to contain it.

"Hold on, Afon." I kept my tone as cool as possible given the mess on the table and the fact he was calling *again*.

Leave me alone, Afon.

"Okay," I heard him say, even with the phone facedown a

foot or so from the spill.

"I spilled tea. Hold on." I was sort of yelling so he might hear. He did.

The muffled, facedown voice said, "Okay." Then he laughed.

After I found a hand towel and mopped up my mess, I snapped up the phone. The back of it still felt slightly damp. "What's up?"

Keep your voice level like you don't care.

"Have you seen the news?"

Boy, oh, boy. Just jump right in, will ya, Afon? And I refused to say, *about the foot?* And instead said, "I was just reading when you called."

"I sure would like to see that foot."

"God, Afon."

Just hang up!

He chuckled but then added, "You know, *I* could tell if there was foul play...afoot!" He laughed at his own lame joke and at my expense.

"I'm sure they have *experts* for that." Why was I engaging him? Why was I emphasizing certain words? "By the way, Afon, it's my husband you're joking about."

Afon had been a successful orthopedic surgeon in Seattle before retiring to our islands. He was single after one failed marriage, but at fifty-eight, he could pass for someone in his late forties. Something he liked to flaunt at the book club meetings. Always wearing a tighter than necessary shirt to show off his arms and tighter than necessary pants to show off his *athletic* form. It had always niggled at me that someone—and in Afon's case, the only guy in the club—would come to the meetings trying to look sexy. I mean, we read in sweatpants and a tee shirt, right? And it seemed to bother me more lately since we bumped into each other on a run that day.

He was now telling me how he was able to determine if an appendage was severed or torn from the body and I just...

wanted… him… to *shut up*! He could be so flipping insensitive.

"Why don't you go ask to help if you're so curious?"

"Hmm." He was actually considering my suggestion. He went silent while he thought about the prospects—his garden variety repartee, spilling over with his special brand of wit, stalling.

Before I could stop myself, I said, "Might be…*fun* for you."

You freak of nature.

"Maybe I will."

Of course, you will.

He went on, "So…you okay? Need anything? *Comp*any?"

Oh. God. Please. I should have been an actor.

"No. I'm good. Thanks. I just want to, uh…"

"Wait?"

"I guess."

"How long?"

"God, Afon. It's only been three months."

"You think there's a chance he's still alive?"

"Who knows?"

Three months. Could time hang up that long without finding his body? Pain burned behind my eye sockets. I wanted desperately to stop thinking about him lying under a rock in a watery grave. But with the foot showing up on shore…that's what everyone would expect. Right?

"You think there's a chance he's not and if not, do you think there's a chance, well, you and me?"

"Look." The word came out sharp. "I have to go," I said, and ended the call without saying goodbye.

I called Liv. She could always talk me down.

Was Afon simply trying to help me feel better? If he was, he had a stupid way of showing it. He didn't need to be so pushy.

Part of me wished *he* were dead and not Larry.

CHAPTER 5
THEN—June 20, 2020

Can you keep our secret, Larry? We have so many secrets between us.

Earlier that morning, Jamie read on *Wunderground.com* that the moon was in its final phase of the month. She hated driving in the dark. An enlarging, brown cataract—one the eye doc had never quite seen the color of before—was growing, causing fireworks to flash and halo around every object she viewed with that eye. She placed a hand over the eye and drove using only the left eye. The left eye worked great, but she worried about peripheral vision so brought her hand back to the steering wheel and slowed her speed.

Waning crescent, the article stated, that the sunset, that final light, would be pinched out after nine that evening. When she arrived home, a worm of orange slithered to nonexistence in the western sky marking nighttime here in Friday Harbor with day somewhere so many miles out into the ocean she could only imagine its vast waters. No land. A voice spoke to her, a long-ago voice from high school geography class, the tip of Australia lay directly opposite from where she stood on her front deck.

Will you keep our secret, Larry? Will anyone find you?

Rob and the deputy kept their voices low. Everyone stopped speaking, stopped moving, *breathing* when the grumble of a large vehicle turned into their three hundred feet of road, stopping before it reached the fork in the circular drive—a decision to go left, this way or that, to the right. The driver killed the engine before choosing. He kept a set of high beams on. The beam skewed the edges between light and dark spotlighting everything in its path—the tar of the drive and trunks of two out of four sweet maple trees growing inside the drive's grassy circle.

Within seconds fumes from the diesel engine reached the porch. A cool summer breeze chilled sweat that had settled on her neck.

She wanted a glass of wine so bad she actually tasted it on her dry lips. A mosquito stung her, and she swatted it.

As her eyes adjusted to a yin and yang of light and dark, the words SAN JUAN COUNTY SEARCH & RESCUE came into focus emblazoned across the rectangle of the truck's side panel. If they thought to, they could repurpose its hulk into a train car or an RV.

"S&R's here," Rob said, calling back to her to fill the stopgap of their conversation.

Jamie checked the time on her cell. It was almost eight fifty p.m. It had been twenty minutes since Rob and his small crew had shown. Nearly an hour since she'd returned home.

How many hours since he...?

Another damn mosquito. She slapped her ear at its buzzing. The bloodsuckers loved humidity. A bat zipped near but thought better when it sensed a larger obstacle, her body, near where its sonar picked up on the mosquito.

Could the bat smell her blood? Could it smell her fever?

Rob hopped back up onto the deck. Ever energetic Rob.

"I gotta deal with this."

Jamie nodded and he hopped back down. His mirth contrasted with the trouble at hand.

She brushed it off to being in charge. He was the mouthpiece this evening. He asserted his authority over the situation and let everyone know.

Jamie followed him but lagged behind, thinking it might be

better to wait rather than encroach on their conversation. He seemed to sense her behind him and turned back, put up his hands for her to stop, then joined the rest of them.

And they all jumped into a flurry of activity.

Everyone moving.

A woman and a man jumped from inside the front of the S&R behemoth, then two more from the back. They all shook hands with Rob.

Niceties? At a time like this?

Rob turned and called to Jamie. "What was he wearing?"

She yelled back, "Oh, uh. I'm not sure. Hold on." The question stumped her. How wasn't she prepared for a question like that? She'd seen this a thousand times on TV. Of *course*, they would need to know what Larry was wearing. "Wait," she said. "Um. A pair of khaki shorts and a black tee shirt." Then added, "A polo."

"Has this ever happened before?" the S&R woman yelled.

"No."

Did she answer too quickly?

Jamie didn't want to mention how Larry sometimes slipped out of the house when she was upstairs, or when she was in the shower.

The woman must have sensed something off and said, "No?" Like Jamie was lying.

"Not like this."

"Like *what* then?"

Pushy bitch.

"Not like this."

Too defensive. Tone it down.

"Never at night," Jamie said. "I mean, he sometimes slips out when I'm not watching him." The statement sounded as though she were talking about a dog or a...a child. "To go look at his lawnmower. Or the car. It doesn't start. It sat too long."

The Porsche was a birthday gift for Larry's seventieth but within a year, she wouldn't allow him to drive. "If they sit too long, they have a security mechanism, I guess. It shuts down, prevents the engine from kicking into gear." She was rambling now. "He can't drive anyway. I drive him, us, everywhere."

Shut up. Shut up.

"He has dementia?"

"It's up in the air. I mean, well, I'm not sure. Some days he's better. Doctors aren't calling it that yet, but they aren't ruling it out either."

"What about today?" she asked.

"Today?"

"How was he today?"

Jamie shook her head, but reversed by saying, "Not bad." Her shoulders lifted ever so slightly, and she wanted to cry.

"Not bad?"

"Not bad. Not great but not terrible either. Not *bad*."

Leave me alone! Aren't you supposed to be searching and rescuing?

Rob and the woman snuck a look between them. Rob said something prompting the other three to gather supplies out of the truck. Two of them slung on their backpacks. The gear inside clattered.

"Ma'am," the woman said, "can you please get an extra set of clothing when we find him?"

Jamie turned away.

When they find him...

But her cell phone rang. She pulled it out of her back pocket. It was Liv.

Jamie turned to check the crew. Their attention was on her.

"Hey Liv. Not now." She turned away and headed inside so they couldn't hear. "Search & Rescue's here. I can't talk." Jamie hung up without hearing Liv's response. She would call her later.

Her feet took each stair up fast. She counted the fourteen steps to the landing and then fifteen, seventeen...twenty-one to the closet. She grabbed a pair of his sweats, a pair of socks, another tee shirt, and a pair of rubber slip-ons.

She hated outing him this way, but she also grabbed a pair of protective briefs too. She didn't know why she insisted on calling them briefs. Yes, they were diapers. But she refused to say the word in front of Larry. So as not to let on about his incontinence. So as not to offend his sense of pride. He still held onto dignity.

She stuffed everything in a recyclable grocery bag.

By the time she got down the stairs and back to them, the detectives and S&R were deciding on teams and which team was to take what direction.

"Here," she said, and handed the clothing to the woman.

"Great. Okay. So, you just need to wait here."

"On the deck?" The question sounded ridiculously helpless.

"There or in the house." Looks, again, exchanged between everyone. "We'll come in when we find him." She was keeping a positive spin on things.

"Just come straight in," Jamie said. "I mean, no need to knock."

"Yes, ma'am."

One of the guys wearing a backpack walked ahead but called back, "AED!"

"Check!" the woman responded.

Jamie understood the acronym. AED—automated external defibrillator.

And all at once, they dispersed, flashlights blazing under the moonless night.

CHAPTER 6
NOW—September 21, 2020

Lying there. His head askew. Are you breathing, Larry?

Often, I awoke only to find Larry in a state of breathless apnea. I needed to stop envisioning him this way.

"I can't get him out of my head," I whispered, choking the words out.

Liv kept her voice low. I assumed Paul was nearby. "I need to call you back," she said. "I can't talk."

"Don't bother. It's the same thing, different day, hour, minute. Call when you can."

Liv had been a friend, a close friend, since we first met after she moved to the island. We hit it off right away. I'll never understand why or how it happened but the trust between us was immediate, was there at our initial meeting.

She called me needing information on how insurance claims work when there's bodily injury in an accident. After determining the kind of accident—auto, home, earthquake, flood—I explained my process and then set her up to talk with Rob, who, if there were any questions about the validity of an accident—in other words, if it looked suspicious, say—could take over in his authority.

Liv was writing a new crime thriller set on the island. We met for coffee and stayed for lunch. I told her, without naming any locals' names, several of our juicier insurance claims. As a claims adjuster and investigator, I work hand in hand with the sheriff's office. I had more pull within the department back then and could help her out a little with getting her questions answered or getting access to closed cases. Some of which were unbelievable, like the Ruby Nester case where she ended up killing her husband, but that one wasn't an insurance claim. That was out-and-out crime. Still, insurance is always involved at some level.

But we did have one Liv liked a lot because, even after files were charged, even after the person was indicted, found guilty, and sentenced, it left people wondering if the defendant was truly guilty. The unanswered question of is he or is he not guilty deepening interest to the community. Liv figured it would play well fictionalized. There was a ton of circumstantial evidence and incredible bits of trace evidence that linked the guy to his girlfriend's "alleged" accident. Her blood alcohol was through the roof; the ME found methamphetamines in her liver tissue. Everything pointed to her getting into a car and driving it off the road into a ravine, where it flipped, landing on its roof. She wasn't wearing a seat belt. Her neck broke instantly.

The trace evidence was the boyfriend's handprint on the window and doorframe, another one on the gear shift set to drive, and a muddy shoe print on the gas pedal.

The prosecutor figured the boyfriend had placed the girl in the car, revved the engine with his shoe, and then set the car into gear before throwing the door closed when the car rolled forward.

It was a clunker of a car anyway. Didn't have all the preventive controls newer cars have—gear and steering wheel locking. That sort of thing. Plus, the boyfriend's leg was injured the same night the girlfriend died in the crash.

Liv ate this story up. She dug in like a shovel into mud. We met often and talked a lot about that case, noting how the evidence pointed to the boyfriend and "what if" he'd done this instead, or that? You know, to avoid suspicion. But she never let me forget, police always suspect the spouse or significant other first. After they flesh out where they were the night of the incident, if they have a decent alibi, the police will move on to the next person of interest.

Liv pored over the photos I took, photos of the bent-up car, the road where it went off the road, the girl's body. Rob had called me in on that one. Normally, as an insurance investigator, I don't see the bodies, but Rob wanted me to take the photos. He'd said his photographer wasn't able to show up before the medical personnel intended to remove her, pronounce her, and take her to the morgue. His call came in after one thirty in the morning. After bars closed giving the chance of an accident more validity. Drinking and driving being the immediate reason for the accident. That is until they checked her liver toxicity which showed no alcohol and after CSI came back with strange data about the car, the brake, the trace prints.

After, Rob wrapped me into several other crime scene investigations. I got to know the procedure well enough to supply Liv with lots of details she needed for her novels. We became close because of her novels and my work.

So, the day S&R came out to the house, when she called me back, I was in a full-on freak out. I understood how law enforcement would proceed, with their suspicious eyes on me. Would they gather enough circumstantial evidence to find me guilty? Even if I were innocent? You never know.

Of course, Liv, in her calming way, talked me down off that ledge. She reminded me that he'd "gone missing." Then nudged me with, "Remember?"

And I did remember. I remembered every single detail about that night.

Larry asked me once, "What's wrong with me?" That was about a year before.

For some reason, he'd stopped using his left arm. He barely swung it when we walked. He held it flaccid like a strand of thick pappardelle hanging there by his hip whether he was sitting on the couch (which was all he did anymore) or walking up and down the stairs.

Then, another of Larry's symptoms emerged. Out of the blue, Larry's nose would drain like someone tapped a spigot. Snot would pour out. He would only stand there, bent slightly forward, not trying to stop it or reach for a tissue. He didn't do anything. He froze with snot spilling onto his lap or the floor or the ground outside, if we were out for a walk.

He waited for me to help, to grab a wad of tissue and wipe his nose.

It got to the point that I had to instruct him how to blow his nose.

"No, Larry. Really blow. Like a honker." Mostly, he would sniffle because he couldn't remember how to blow his own nose. I wasn't sure what was going on so, instead of going to our family doc, we went to his cardio doc. The heart doc told us that he was retaining fluids and had a thoracic aortic *aneurism*.

Then, the heart doc put him on diuretics to bleed off any extra water he was retaining. He had fluid around his heart. And within six months, his ankles swelled. Even on the diuretics. Then came the diagnosis. His dementia would be an issue. No ethical surgeon would operate because the anesthesia would turn what was left of his brain into vegetable soup.

The heart doc went onto say that without the surgery, he had three to five years to live. His ticking heart valve coupled with the ticking clock sounded like a death gong.

The aortic aneurism would burst, a widow-maker, the doc had said, and Larry would die. Like my friend's husband, Brian.

One time, Larry ended up wedged in a tight spot near the toilet. He had bent down to pick up his diapers.

Then, he fell off the bed. Not falling hard like falling after tripping. More like a slow slide onto the floor and getting stuck, sitting there on his ass.

We purchased a bedrail.

After that came a hospital bed. They call them "split-Kings,"

I guess to soften the blow.

He liked his side elevated. I liked my side flat. Two sheet sets for each side of the king.

I had been fooling myself, thinking that this was some weird blip for Larry. That he would snap out of it. I wouldn't let myself believe Larry had dementia. Not until we got the hospital bed. That's when denial stepped aside and realization took hold.

This was happening. Larry was either going to die from the dementia—a slow diminishing crawl toward the end. Or he would go out with a bang, with his heart exploding and although fast, with a great deal of pain.

I prayed a lot back then. For Larry to avoid what the doctors were foretelling.

I prayed to God that Larry's death would be painless and quick and that he wouldn't be scared.

But who gets all three? Still, I prayed and prayed Larry got all three.

The weird thing is Larry's dementia wasn't always horrible. There were special times. The dearest of times when Larry would ask: *Did I ever tell you...?*

And it could be anything.

Did I ever tell you about Jimmy Johnson?

Did I ever tell you about my trip to Paris?

Did I ever tell you how Brent (his brother) and I climbed Mount Rainier?

I would answer accordingly. I mean, I wasn't going to lie if I'd heard the story before and I'd say something like, "Wasn't that when...?"

If I didn't know, I would say, "I don't think so?" But then those times also became repeat topics of Larry's. And other times, even if I'd already heard one of his stories, I wouldn't stop him from telling me again. He found great joy in his memories. And greater joy telling me about them. Showing me that he remembered something, anything inside that sweet head of his.

He wanted me to know that he remembered things. Remembering was important to Larry. And because remembering was important to him, it was important to me.

Larry's dementia was different from my mother's Alzheimer's. And hadn't it been Larry who helped me with my mom back then? He was fine only three years ago.

Three years.

Those years skipped by so fast. And yet, today, three years ago feels like decades.

The switch to dementia in Larry's brain flipped to the on position as suddenly as someone flipping off a light. He was bright one moment. And the next? The lights blinked out.

We were still grieving the loss of my mom.

I felt hoodwinked. As if some evil cosmic force had me in its crosshairs.

It didn't seem fair. Mother's illness to death inched along, minute by minute.

Larry and I had been taking care of her in one way or another, on and off, for thirteen years until she died in 2016.

After, we made plans, talking about how we might enjoy the rest of our time together.

Then, boom. Larry got the dementia diagnosis.

I felt gypped. *Gypped*. A word I hadn't used since I was a kid. It was as though God were rebuking me.

But why? And I knew. For my thoughts, that my mother was a burden, *that's* why.

Honor thy father and thy mother.

Something like that. One of the ten commandments. How children should obey and love them no matter what, right? Yes. That's the rule. And if they sinned against their parents, God would smite the children for those sins.

But was God a vengeful God?

Hell, yes. I remember instances in the Bible when he exacted punishment on people for sinning. Think Noah's Ark, the Tower of Babel. And the biggie: Sodom and Gomorrah.

My sister, Mel, told me once that God was "teaching," but I understood "teaching" to mean punishing me.

She said, "He's teaching you compassion."

Please. And this coming from the woman who had hired an attorney to try and null Mom's will so that she got the house, the retirement accounts, and the safety deposit box full of her mother's finest jewelry.

Mel had long since fallen out of favor with Mother, and yet, she had the nerve to lecture me on compassion. We don't see into our own mirrors clearly, do we?

Mel was furious when, after Mom died, the will appointed me as executor of her estate. Not only that, but the will also distributed most of Mom's assets to me.

Eventually, Mel backed off the lawyer idea. It didn't matter. Mom was loaded. There were enough funds, properties, and diamonds to keep us both comfortable until we died.

And now, with Larry's condition, the need for a part-time caregiver, for all the extraneous medical bills, medical equipment, and diapers, the extra money is, dare I say, a *God*send.

And oh how I worried, during the timespan of Larry's disappearance and when he'd been presumed dead, that no one would pose the question I dreaded most:

Why didn't you hire someone to watch Larry the night he went missing?

So far, no one *had* asked. Not yet anyway.

CHAPTER 7
THEN—June 20, 2020

Why do I care what anyone thinks?

Denial is not a river in Egypt.

Denial is a place where we go to visit the past.

Denial is a game played in one's own head.

Jamie knew he was dead. She'd seen people on the news whose loved ones had gone missing. She saw how they sensed their family members were either alive or were dead.

"I just knew she was alive." Some would say after finding their daughter or sister.

But others would say, "I just knew she was dead." This only after finding the body.

Jamie knew Larry was dead. Still, she'd talked herself into believing, taking a dive into magical thinking, that they would find him. That they might bring him back to her, walk him into the house, and she could wrap her arms around him and stay there, holding him once more.

She could feed his body next to hers. Give him something warm to drink. Feed him his dinner. It had been hours since his last meal.

When the crew returned, Jamie was putting things away—a dirty plate from Larry's lunch, the crusts from her own grilled cheese sandwich, and a blue bottle of dish soap among a few smaller things she couldn't name now to save her life.

She'd already sprayed the counter with sanitizer and stowed a couple utensils still in the sink, left there before flying out to get to the book club meeting.

But what else are you supposed to do with your time while S&R searches for your missing spouse? Just wait around, drumming your fingertips until they're bloody? And then what?

Giving up on caring *what* they thought, Jamie poured herself a glass of wine, a glass Larry had set out for her while she was scrambling to make it in time for the meeting. That was before the fight.

And if you can't have a glass of wine at a time like this, then when?

Later, Rob would bring up that she'd been "hiding things." Three months later, to be exact, when he returned to tell her the investigation had led them to possibly consider their house as a crime scene.

Earlier that day, before she left for the book club, Larry had been watching MSNBC. Now, the news was airing journalists and reporters wearing masks for protection against COVID-19, explaining how the infection was spreading like "wildfire," they said. In another segment, reporters spoke with a woman whose son had been killed by a cop. Her shirt read, "I Can't Breathe." Behind the mother, thousands of people wore similar shirts and masks. Some held signs reading BLACK LIVES MATTER with others reading GET OFF MY NECK. One said FUCK TRUMP which surprised Jamie that they caught the image on film and didn't censor it.

The live footage was being shot in DC in front of the White House and it was getting dark there—three hours later than the west coast. They were still protesting, and it was edging up on midnight east coast time and nine p.m. where Jamie stood staring at the news. Part of her taking it in while the other part of her was suspended in disbelief that Larry was dead. They wouldn't say that yet. They would have to find him, his body to go to the extreme of pronouncing him dead. Right now, they would only refer to Larry as a missing person.

While she stared into the monitor, Jamie recalled how strange it was to see everyone in masks. But six months later, it felt stranger to see people without masks. Like they were sinning, breaking the law that way.

Everyone at the book club donned a mask. All businesses and public places in Friday Harbor required them upon entry. The library was no different. She remembered feeling relieved when they reopened the library because she worried about homeless people. They tended to congregate there, inside and out, to use the bathroom or just come in from the weather. She worried about one gal in particular who had gotten help from Jamie at the church when she was a deacon.

Larry had strapped the simple blue medical mask he usually wore longways onto a bottle of wine he had placed on the end table like the wine bottle needed protection from COVID too.

He'd drunk one glass of wine. His glass was lying on its side.

It didn't seem unusual because Larry was always knocking things over, spilling things, peeing on the floor. He would unroll an entire roll of toilet paper and leave it on the floor with only a shred hanging onto the cardboard tube.

So, for Jamie, the wine glass on its side was just another mess of his she needed to clean up. She heard him bump around from upstairs when she was slipping on her shoes. Something was always falling, spilling, dropping, or breaking. She called out asking if he was okay.

"I'm fine," he yelled up to her.

A small pool of red liquid spilled out and dribbled off the end table and onto the floor.

She hadn't gotten to that area of the room when S&R returned. The wine glass had only a teaspoon of wine inside after tipping over. Jamie's bottle of water still sat where she left it on her side of the table. She hadn't taken a sip.

Larry typically set out a glass of wine for her for when she returned from book club meetings. Even in his addled state, he still remembered that they enjoyed sharing wine together in the evenings. He started early, and because he did, he thought she might like a glass too.

She left the door unlocked for S&R when they returned. She expected to hear them come in when they returned but did not.

"What are you doing?" Rob said. He was alone inside the kitchen.

Jamie jumped and whirled around at the sound of his voice. "Did you find anything? I mean, is he with you?" She slipped her mask back over her mouth.

She couldn't read his expression from only his eyes, which appeared as a mix of humor and horror all at the same time. Then, he shook his head, no.

"What?" she said. "What's wrong?"

He shook his head, refusing to respond. He had taken off his shoes. Probably left them at the door. That's why she didn't hear him. That, and because her head was in a completely different universe with so many imaginings and fears, so many thoughts set inside horrific scenarios.

He sidled further into the kitchen near the counter, where two barstools sat under the counter's thick, pink-veined granite.

Within seconds, the rest of the search team piled inside the front door, thumping their booted feet into the den. A trail of mud and pine needles dropped from their shoes, the scent of the woods following them in like a loyal dog after its master. Their gear clanked around their belts and shoulders. Jamie glanced at Rob. He'd removed most of his gear along with his boots. Had he been trying to sneak up on her?

When everyone got into the den, Lester, Jamie's cat, scrambled off the chair from under the table where he'd been sleeping and zoomed into the laundry room.

"You didn't find anything?" Jamie asked.

"Tissue," one of the guys said.

"Carter," the woman hushed him.

"Tissue? Like tissue paper?" Jamie asked.

The woman shook her head. "No, not tissue paper. Tissue," she said, and slung her mask under her chin. She stood out from the other men. In the light of the room, Jamie noticed that she wore lipstick and mascara. Jamie lightly swept her fingers against the mask over her own dry lips. Rarely did she wear lipstick; mostly for book club and Zoom talks.

"Should we be wearing masks?" Jamie asked. Her mind bounced from thought to thought.

"We've all tested negative."

So, no?

Jamie said, in response, "We've been self-quarantining since the news broke in February. We rarely go out. Went out," she said, using past tense about she and Larry. "We've stockpiled for the apocalypse." It was supposed to make things lighter, to be a joke but her words came off inappropriate for the moment.

Am I supposed to ask them if they would like water?

"Would you like some water?"

"No, ma'am," Rob said. He was assuming the same tone as the gal.

"Ma'am," she said. "This is what we know." She relayed details of the search. Words that siphoned up into Jamie's consciousness but then bobbed away like driftwood over water. Her badge read *Elizabeth*. Jamie sensed that Elizabeth carried some sort of rank over all these men. She continued explaining with Rob injecting additional information he felt important to add.

Bottom line? They hadn't found Larry. Just the tissue. As it turns out, Larry's tissue, skin tissue.

Elizabeth questioned Jamie about the crevice.

Had it always been there?

Jamie nodded, then added, "Since before she bought the land." Both the questions and answers felt surreal, like she'd dropped acid and was trying to stay upright inside a spiral cakewalk.

Rob noted that someone should *really* cover that up.

Meaning, *she* should.

Elizabeth's eyes scanned Jamie, scanned the room, scanned the floor.

"The crevice," Jamie said, her eyes bounced from person to person, finally landing on Rob. "Did you go into it?"

He shook his head, no.

"That's the thing," Elizabeth said, "we don't have spelunking gear. We can get some tomorrow, but we can't get down there."

Down there.

Elizabeth's gear clanked when she moved toward the spot where Larry normally sat.

But Jamie was keyed into hearing about the crevice. "Could you see anything inside?" Her hand came up to her throat.

Rob said, "We couldn't see the bottom."

"Did you yell? I mean, did you call his name?"

Glances flitted between them.

"Yes, ma'am," Elizabeth said. "We called. No one answered."

Elizabeth knelt onto the floor. "This blood?" she asked.

Rob stepped nearer where Elizabeth inspected.

"Oh, I didn't see that," Jamie said. "He knocked over a glass of wine. It's wine."

"Where's the glass?" Elizabeth said.

"In the dishwasher." Jamie pointed at the appliance and felt like an idiot like, look this is a dishwasher. And over here, well this here is a stove.

Elizabeth pulled out a swab and dipped it into the wine. Then she smelled it. She nodded to Rob that, *yes*, it was wine. She stood up again and walked into the kitchen. Jamie grabbed the rag from the sink, moved out of Elizabeth's way, sidling near the stainless-steel refrigerator, then passed her and mopped the wine with the rag.

Jamie went back to the subject of the crevice. "Do you think he's in the crevice?"

Rob took in a deep breath and frowned. When he looked at her, she thought he might be angry or simply didn't want to discuss the matter with her.

He turned his attention to Elizabeth. It was obvious he didn't want to speak about it.

"*Do* you, Rob?" she demanded.

The dishwasher door clicked open. In her peripheral, Elizabeth was holding up the glass, inspecting it. She pulled a baggy out of pocket and dropped the glass inside. Then clicked the dishwasher closed again.

With Rob's attention now back on Jamie, he answered her, "We dropped a fist-sized rock into it." He stopped and made a face like he was going to be sick.

"And?"

"It fell a good ways." Someone coughed. "You could hear it bouncing off the crevice wall. You know, against rocks and stuff. Then it," he paused. He checked Elizabeth's face.

"Then it *what*?"

Elizabeth jumped in. "We heard it bounce off something then," she paused, her eyes batting between the men, "then, a splash."

CHAPTER 8
NOW—September 21, 2020

Please God, make all this stop.

Again, yet another call came shortly after Afon's. By the way, Afon was getting too cozy with the idea of calling whenever he wanted. I needed to put a stop to it.

This call was from Rob Rimmler. I expected someone from the courthouse to call after reading the article.

"We need you to come down and identify," Rob said. He paused, then continued, "the shoe."

I must have made a sound that I understood although don't remember doing so. I froze and my skin went cold. My internal thermometer flip-flopped to blazing as though a demon was playing games with my temperature on-off switch.

"Where? I mean, the sheriff's office?" I asked.

"The coroner's office," he said.

The coroner's office.

It sounded so final. This was it then. If the shoe belonged to Larry, they would make the determination. They would officially record his death. I knew this process. I'd seen it play out with insurance clients.

I bit the inside of my cheek so hard, I tasted blood. Rob must have heard the strain in my voice because he got quieter when he spoke, showed a bit of compassion.

"Look, Jamie," he said. "If it is, you know, Larry's, at least there will be some closure."

But the words didn't comfort me much. The blood tasted like iron. My cheek burned.

I reacted badly.

"Closure? From a *shoe*!?" I laughed, laughed at his audacity. It came out cold and icy. My words smoldered with anger, with sadness.

"Jamie, I...I don't know what to say. We just need you to come down. Sooner than later."

My arms went limp. Had I been shoveling rocks? I lowered the phone and paused to gather my emotions.

Finally, I said, "Give me an hour?"

"That'll be fine," he said.

And we ended our call.

But another one came in fast. It was Liv.

"Hey," she said. "I just saw the story. Are you okay?"

"I have to go down to the coroner's office."

"God."

"*You're* invoking God?" Liv could tell I was trying to make a joke. "A recent yet devout atheist?"

"Right?" I heard air sift into the phone when she chuckled.

Then, silence fell between us, a silence we used as part of our communication, a communication we didn't need words for.

Finally, Liv broke the lull. "Look, *James*. You need a ride or anything? Just name it."

"Aw, thanks, Liv, but I think I need to do this one on my own."

I figured she would ask. Like any good author, seeing the shoe that he'd been wearing the night he went missing would make for great fodder in her next bestseller. However, Larry's memory needed protection over some desire to gather information for something fictional. This was as real as it got. I wasn't about to let this scene play out for anyone but me and I certainly never wanted to read about it some novel. Even Liv's.

All at once, a cruel tightness wrapped around my chest.

"Ohmygod, Liv. I'm so sad."

He was gone. Really gone. There was no more denying. No more maybes. Realization locked me in its tight grip. People think grief is a mental state but it's physical too. It punches you about the head and gut when you least expect it and then shakes you by the shoulders only when it feels you're ready to finally handle the truth.

And the pain...the pain is so intense, so all encompassing, like a vise grip around the heart.

We both knew Larry was dead. *We* knew it.

That fact lay in a fierce backdrop in Liv's voice, in her eyes every time we met. In her actions of late. That fierceness was in my own heart. The knowledge, red and inflamed, fiercely surrounding my heart, at every beat.

Liv broke the silence first. "Has Gigi called? Or Steph?"

"Not yet."

Again, silence.

"Maybe they haven't seen the story," she said.

I made a hissing sound. How could they not know about this? A story that would rage through the island's grapevine. It was the biggest news since Gigi's husband died ten years before. "Maybe."

"I know. And hey. You know, you don't have to go tomorrow." She meant to the book club.

Was there hope in her statement? Did she want me to miss the book club meeting?

"You don't want me to?" I said.

"It's not that."

I'd missed the last two but swore to her I would attend September's because the group decided to read Liv's latest bestselling novel, *The Baggy Edge of Thighs*, a light, humorous read about two women who sometimes swap out each other's clothing, women's fiction.

"No. I'm going." I hesitated. "Is that okay? I mean, if you don't want me to, I won't?"

"No, it's not like that at all, nothing like that." She coughed, then said, "It's just, you know, well, we'll understand if you don't want to or if you decide at the last minute to not come. You know that, right? I mean, God, Jamie, this story, having to go to the coroner's, and all. You get what I mean, don't you?"

"Yeah. I do. But I read your book. It was like the one joyful thing that happened during these last three months. I want to discuss it because I thought it was, well, awesome."

Liv chuckled, her breath hitting the receiver's mic.

I continued, "That, of course. But also, because I want to be the one to tell everyone about, well, you know...the *shoe*." Of course, Liv knew I meant *foot*. Everyone had heard a human foot had washed up at South Beach from the news. I wouldn't say foot. I continued, "You know. Before, well, before everyone has a chance to hear it secondhand."

"I *totally* get that." I loved Liv's thirty-something style of phrasing, her word choice. Interestingly, that voice was absent from her writing. She became someone else in her books, her second self. We all have a second self. Call it the lightest case of schizophrenia, call it a persona, but we all have secret selves who help us cope, who fight for us, who act a certain way in public from how we act in private. Liv's second self was obvious in her books. With me, however, Liv was her real self. And I was my real self with Liv.

So, I should have expected but was caught off-guard when she offered help. She said, "You know, James. If you need, anything, *anything* at all...you know, like a shoulder. I'm here, Jamesies."

My voice quavered. I swallowed but could only get out a whisper. "Thanks," I said, and hung up fast before she could say another word and before I completely lost it.

CHAPTER 9
THEN—June 20, 2020

Search & Rescue would exit her property a hair after ten o'clock that evening, leaving Rob behind to finish. Under a severe contrast of porch light and black night, Jamie stood, hands gripping her upper arms, each arm wrapped across the other. Rob had pocketed his notes, keeping his hands pressed deep inside both pants pockets. The red-and-white checkered hankie snuck out the back pocket. She wanted to snatch it, yank it out, try to steal it without him knowing.

What kind of person was she turning into?

"Well," he said.

With Jamie's attention broken, with him leaving the word hanging there with no place to go, Jamie too said, "Well."

Jamie nodded when their eyes connected, hers darting away, suddenly interested in the S&R truck's engine thrumming to life. Diesel fuel floated up to the porch and hung in the air. The odor remained after the big truck faded from view. Only its red bumper lights evidence that it had ever been there at all. The trace of oily diesel left behind like unwanted afterbirth.

Jamie's flesh prickled. She smoothed both hands over her skin, sending the prickling back into slumber. The temperature had cooled down since everyone arrived more than two hours before.

As Search & Rescue exited, a second vehicle she assumed

was driven by one of the first responders who had arrived with Rob, somewhere out on the road, rumbled to life. However, instead of driving away, the sound of the car's engine got closer. Soon, its headlamps broke through. The car was smaller. As it approached, the lights broke onto the driveway through a screen of trees and shrubs. The car's lights fanned out onto the ground and bounced off a garbage dumpster. As the car passed by, the dumpster's chalky blue color, a sudden patch tucked within a camouflage of shrubbery went black again as its lights glanced away from the container as if the lights themselves were pointing to items in the crime scene—here is a tree, here is a driveway, here is a dumpster—as proof there existed any life amid all the darkness.

Once the vehicle came into full view, Jamie recognized it. It was Liv.

"Of course," Rob said under his breath.

Jamie stiffened but didn't respond to his comment. How long had she been parked there?

Jamie let her eyes slide to Rob's face. He squinted. His chin set hard, the muscles along his jawline twitched, exhibiting his mood.

Liv pulled in behind Rob's vehicle and parked. The interior light blinked on when she opened the door. She got out and stood, leaving the door open.

The air went dead between them, a good sixty feet of dead air.

Jamie spoke first. "Hey Liv. Rob's just finishing up here. Aren't you, Rob?" Her hands made vise grips on her biceps. She knew they would bruise by tomorrow.

"Yep," he said. He flashed an angry look at Jamie. "Just leaving."

He lowered his voice. His face went stiff. His words cut short. "Be in touch," he said, and then, "Tomorrow." Like it was a threat.

Liv closed her car door.

Rob turned up his intercom speaker. His gear rattled with each step down off the porch. How was it she hadn't heard him enter the house earlier? His radio crackled to life.

Liv and Rob passed one another within thirty feet of the porch, each slowing their pace but not stopping.

Rob said, "Liv." And tapped the brim of an imaginary hat.

Liv said, "Rob." She kept her eyes focused on Jamie, not glancing once in his direction.

But Rob stopped and turned back.

"Hey Liv," he said, his words meant to stop her, a command for her to turn.

Liv's posture slumped and she stopped. By that point, his skin was graying out under the dimness. Still, Jamie could make out a reflection from the porchlights lasering onto his irises.

Liv turned to him with all the effort it would take for two infants to turn an elephant. Neither said a word until Rob spoke. "Writing anything interesting these days?"

Liv only nodded. She rubbed her arms.

Rob went on. His voice goading. "Anything about missing persons?" His smile was evident, even from the porch. But he wasn't joking.

Jamie's heart heaved inside her chest.

Liv didn't respond. She ignored his question and headed up the entry steps to meet Jamie.

Rob called out again, "Here about this from the dispatch radio, did ya, Liv? 'Cause you have amazing timing. You know, showing up here and all."

When Liv got up onto the porch, she said, "Come on." Then she pulled Jamie by the waist and led her back inside.

CHAPTER 10
NOW—September 21, 2020

God, please let this go fast. Rip the bandage off. Please, God.

Surely, polar ice caps charted warmer temperatures than the room they brought me into. And the white interior didn't help warm the place. I expected stainless steel and drab colors. Don't ask me why but I did.

The morgue was a new addition for San Juan County. Randie Keener had been vying for one since I could remember, since before I stepped off the boat in 1997 when I arrived from Phoenix, and since before Larry and I got together. Around the same time Larry broke off whatever he was doing with Randie. He'd said it wasn't serious. But then there was some kerfuffle between them after we started dating. I figured what wasn't serious for Larry *had* been for Randie.

Time has a way of giving you what you want. That is, if you push, and Randie pushed. She was the county PA, prosecuting attorney, but also a hybrid, a lawyer with a medical degree, which is one reason why she qualified for the coroner job.

Typically, in small counties, the powers that be combine duties of the county coroner with those of the prosecuting attorney because the coroner is responsible for investigating *and* certifying the cause of death. Mostly in cases where death was sudden, unexpected, or the result of an accident, or by questionable circumstances—criminal circumstances or some suspected criminal manner.

Because of this investigative arm of the coroner, Randie Keener and other deputies respond twenty-four/seven to a death call, to investigate and answer questions. That's how the local authority functioned. After the initial examination, the coroner would ship the body off to the mainland for further review by an ME, a medical examiner. But Randie's medical degree with a completed residency in her back pocket and a ME fellowship complete with board certification all before moving to the island, she now had a morgue to call her own. A small one, but hey. Who cares?

Anyway, the branch of the morgue they brought us into was a stark room with painted block walls and a concrete floor, one that echoed every noise, even our whispers. Every footfall from my leather soles, every squeak from Rob's too, pinballed across the room hitting every wall, the ceiling, each slatted window. Every motion from the shoosh of pants or shirt sleeve, every human or mechanical movement produced sound. The door's weather stripping against the concrete floor, whirring from four sets of overhead fluorescent lamp ballasts, waves of air lowing inside an exposed venting system all brought the morgue to life. The irony was not lost on me.

The floors had been painted a dull ash hue but gleamed under a high gloss coat of lacquer that caused our shoes to squeak. The white slatted windows refracted light. It brought to mind the view a prisoner view out a jail cell, one at autumn trees going red, orange, and sunny yellow. Everything else was white.

As soon as we entered, we stopped speaking. We stopped whispering. To do so seemed a sin. Breathing became our only communication. That, and the static and chatter from Rob's shoulder radio mic. He lowered the radio, but it still hissed out communications from dispatchers and other deputies and law enforcers on other radios.

Then, boom! Something struck the door.

Both of us yanked to attention, stood from our chairs,

spooked and alert. Randie Keener pushed through the door. I felt a sudden urge to laugh. It was only nerves, of course. My knuckles had gone white from holding my hands so tight against my lips, steeple-style.

Then, it happened. I let only a whisper of a giggle slip out. Rob turned my way. His face serious. His eyes saying, *Shut up.*

But I couldn't. Another giggle slipped out. Why was I acting this way? It had to be nerves.

All the white. It seemed too much and suddenly became unbearable as if I might lift off the floor.

Then entered Randie wearing all white too—tip to toe. From her white hair to her lab coat. She'd pulled her hair into a messy knot and rubber banded it onto the crown of her head, a sticky serving of angel hair pasta. She wore white slacks. And her white tennies squirmed and complained like an old woman.

Randie leaned over the rolling steel table she pushed into the room. She pushed with effort; her body angled out behind the table.

An ore boxcar came to mind. I giggled again. Rob shot another angry look my way.

But the urge to laugh stopped.

Over the center of the table, a white sheet had been slung leaving six inches of stainless steel showing on both ends. From the center of the sheet sprung a lump.

The lump of course was or was not Larry's shoe.

All the white in the room began to gray. The gray grew dingier and was going black.

I stumbled into Rob.

Was I going to faint? I'd never fainted before. Was this what fainting felt like?

But before I blacked out, he caught me by my elbow, cupping one hand on it and the other around my waist. He pulled me into his frame and squeezed me closer.

He was about to help me sit but as he was doing so, something snagged my sweater at the elbow and distracted my thoughts. His finger, the same one he'd hurt the night Larry went missing, was set in an aluminum finger brace.

"Sorry," he said, about snagging my sweater and worked to pull the brace free, then eased me down into the chair and sat next to me.

"Your finger's not better?"

Why am I whispering?

"'S'nothin'." He was whispering too. "Needs an operation." And he waved off the injury, waving off my concerns the same way he had three months before.

Randie parked the table in the center of the room. With the toe of her right tennie, she set each brake at the table's wheels. She leaned against a bank of drawers and doors, sat and paused. She set her hands behind her against the counter. Then she said, "It's *very* difficult, Jamie. We understand *this*." I assumed she was reciting these words because I'd nearly passed out. Randie continued, "That, um, this *part* is *very* difficult." She kept emphasizing certain words as though I didn't understand.

But then, maybe Randie was flustered. Or maybe she was embarrassed about before, about Larry and their romantic involvement.

I also had to wonder if this part of her job, this coroner thing, ever got any easier.

An empathetic person would have to think that it did not.

"Just give me a sec. Can you?" I said.

Okay, God. When I asked you to make it go fast, well, I made a mistake. Please. Do not. I repeat. Do not rip off the bandage.

"Take all the time you need," she said.

"Thanks, Randie." *Oh, shoot. Did I need to be formal?* "Ms. Keener. What am I supposed to call you?" I was rambling. Great.

"Randie's fine," she said.

Rob relaxed his back against his chair. His walkie-talkie crackled and clicked. He adjusted the volume to a lower setting again. Why didn't he just turn the damn thing off?

I took in a couple of deep breaths, letting each out as slowly as possible.

Randie glanced away.

Rob touched my shoulder. I slid to the lip of my chair and pressed up. Rob followed my lead and we walked to the steel table together—Rob's hand leading my elbow and the other on my back. Had the room grown wider? It felt as though we walked a mile to where the shoe lay.

I was being ridiculous. How could it be Larry's shoe? He was fully intact last I saw him. It wasn't necessarily Larry's. And that's what I talked myself into.

Fear made me think it was his shoe, but I hoped it wasn't. So, I talked myself into that notion.

It won't be Larry's shoe. You can go home.

But there was that second part of me who wanted to know that it was his. And that the search would be over. Closure. Authorities would deem Larry dead. Which, of course, he was. I *knew* he was.

However, another part of me hoped the shoe…but *wait*, was it just a shoe?

I needed to think, to think back to our phone conversation. Rob had mentioned…hadn't he? That I would be identifying a shoe, right? For whatever reason, I couldn't remember his words.

I stiffened. "Wait," I said, pausing.

Time warped. The room spun. This was going too fast. I suddenly became self-conscious. I mean, did I look the way I felt? Like I was about to freak out?

"Ohmygod," I said. "Is the foot…?" But stopped short of finishing.

Randie's eyes flashed to Rob.

"Oh crap," he said.

Oh crap?

Had he neglected to tell me?

I turned to him. His face had paled. He seemed to fade into the wall behind him.

"It's just a *shoe*. Right?"

I searched Rob's face. He stole his eyes away. I covered my mouth.

"Oh, dear lord," I said. "Wait. Okay. Wait a sec. Wait-wait-wait-wait-wait."

Once again, Rob, who hadn't left my side tried to lead me back to the chair. But I wrenched out of his hold and got there in the nick of time, right before my legs failed me.

My breathing went wacky. Each breath clicked like rapid-fire. I was breathing but was getting no air. So, I sucked in more air. But...nothing. I couldn't breathe.

"Give. Me. A sec."

My voice went thready.

"She's gonna faint, Rob. Don't just stand there watching her. Get a bag," Randie said. She pointed somewhere to the right of Rob. He double-timed to a sink, opened the drawer, crackled open a white paper evidence bag, ran back to me, then placed the bag over my face.

"Breathe," Rob said.

Randie's eyes locked onto mine. We were having an unspoken conversation. Her jaw was set and angry, then she softened. Once again, she shot Rob a look one that someone should have told me that I would be identifying more than just a shoe.

"Take all the time you need, Jamie," she said. But her eyes betrayed her, and she glanced up to the clock.

THE BOOK CLUB—Then & Now

"Come back. Even as a shadow. Even as a dream."
—YourTango.com

CHAPTER 11
THEN—June 20, 2020

We have so little time. Is this all part of a nightmare?

Jamie got the emergency text notification on her phone—an earthquake, a real rumbler charting 6.7 magnitude, had rolled under the island. Another message followed about how to prevent damage to homes. It stated to turn off gas lines at the source, check for pipe breakages in water lines, check water levels often, offered an emergency number with a recorded message and website reiterating how to handle a big earthquake.

She fretted over the checklist and worked to get everything done before leaving for the meeting. She checked on Larry, making sure he had everything he would need in her absence.

That's when he became enraged. It had been a week since the last bout of agitation. That time, he became angry about a TV commercial. This time, he accused her of wanting to *kill* him. These bouts of confusion and frustration, the aggressions, had worsened in the past few months. Jamie upped the quality of their food to leafy greens, and vitamin rich vegetables, fresh fruits, and berries. He hated all of it. Said it was rabbit food and threw his plate at her.

This time, he dogged her, *nip-nip*-nipping at her with his accusations. She refused to listen to him, but he chased her out of the master bathroom, a tirade of hurtful words spewing from him. Then, they were on the landing. But he didn't stop the onslaught. His shoulders tensed and he backed her against the guest room door, pinning her there.

"Larry," Jamie said. "You're scaring me."

An ugly laugh came out of him. "See how it feels?"

"You're being silly. I'm not trying to kill you."

He grabbed the wall and stumbled but leaned harder into her, pressing his full weight against her. A small roller groaned. They had small earthquakes in the past few years but none they felt at the house. So, when she heard the groan, Jamie said, "Is that a jet engine?"

Her question seemed to shake him out of his anger for a moment and he backed off. She noticed one of his feet was too close to the lip of the landing.

"Larry, be careful."

She'd fallen twice before from the top but fortunately only got banged up—bruised her hip, skinned her shins and an elbow, and twisted her shoulder. Fortunately, she didn't break any bones. There was no blood. Nothing to call emergency services about. She limped around for a few days afterward, and she remembered thinking that it was a miracle she didn't kill herself.

"Larry," she said again. But he cut her off. All his rage flooding the blood in his face.

"It's true, isn't it?! Admit it!"

"Larry, you're going to fall."

He wore tennis shoes and had double-knotted the laces. The toe of his left shoe sat an inch off the landing's edge. All his weight was on his left leg. He was so close to a dangerous fall, his body in such a precarious spot so near the stairwell.

"Your foot," she said. But he pushed her back with both hands. The handle of the guest room door jammed into her spine. She might be able to slip inside but she needed to talk him down. She wouldn't leave him in this state unless she was in danger.

She tried again. "Larry, wait."

He raised a hand. He'd never hit her before. Never. The mood swings from happy to hysterical grew out of the dementia. His hand hovered near her cheek. He squinted and set his jaw. Then he fisted his hand.

"No," she said.

He pulled his elbow back but stopped inches before punching her.

He'd never hit her. Never. All the craziness was the dementia.

He began to cry. He closed his eyes.

He turned into a pitiful old man.

She'd been so afraid he would hit her. Her breathing raced and her heart pounded but she calmed her voice.

"Honey, be careful. Step back a little. You're too close to the stairs."

But he must've smelled fear like a hyena cornering its kill.

"Admit it!" he screamed.

Jamie shrank tighter against the door. If she was fast, she could get away from him, lock herself inside the room, and call 9-1-1 if she had to, but she wanted him to calm down. To let the rage pass. He would forget all about it by tomorrow. Hell, maybe even within the hour.

However, as if God was watching their fight, He gave Jamie a way out. Either that or He was testing her.

For a second time, the earth under the house began to moan. But this time it sounded like a banshee crawling up from the earth's core, screeching so close, she covered her ears. Larry's angry face morphed into surprise and then into terror.

The house wobbled. It creaked. It rattled and shimmied.

She felt drunk. She couldn't keep her balance and turned to the door. She grabbed onto the doorknob and pressed the other hand against the jamb.

Larry's face stiffened. He stumbled. His arms flew up once. Her hand jutted out.

His eyes rolled. He grappled for her.

But she pulled back.

The stairwell twisted under the quake.

He flailed again. His eyes filled with terror and sadness. And he reached for her again trying to catch his balance.

But that shoe. That shoe sat so dangerously close to the edge…

CHAPTER 12
THEN—June 20, 2020

"What was that flash?" Jamie had asked Liv. Her nerves were pinballing all over the place. Her emotions, papercuts on each fingertip.

"I didn't see anything," Liv said.

When Jamie stopped pulling, Liv had to stop.

Jamie squinted deep into the woods trying to locate the precise spot but found nothing.

She said, "That's weird. I know I saw something."

"Lightning, maybe?" They stopped only a moment when Liv urged her forward. "We have to finish this."

Jamie's face crumpled. Liv tried to console.

"Jamie." Her voice could soothe Jamie for any number of stressful states of affairs, but not so easily now.

"I can't do it," Jamie said.

"We can't stop here. Look. Jamie, we got this far." She grabbed Jamie's face with care. "The story can't end here. You didn't do anything wrong."

When she released her, Jamie fell back a step. "But how can we..."

"Okay. I can do this part alone. You take a break."

But when Liv got a few yards away, Jamie met up with her and they both bore the weight together.

* * *

Jamie followed Liv in her own car. Before long, Liv had edged farther down the road and was turning out of sight.

After pulling into a spot next to Liv in the library's parking lot, Jamie killed her engine. Liv was already standing outside her car, leaning against the door and fumbling around inside her purse.

The sun sat fat and orange above the tree line. Its rays glowed off Liv's face, making her skin shine in a peach tone. When she looked up, she squinted and dropped a pair of sunglasses from on top of her head to the bridge of her nose.

"Hey," Jamie said.

Liv had found what she was digging around for and presented it, stiff-armed, to Jamie.

"Here. Use these," she said. Liv handed Jamie a bottle of eyedrops, the kind that wipe away all redness.

"Got anything for *swollen* eyes?"

"You're not that bad. Once the red is gone, no one will be able to tell at all. Just tell them you got so scared from the earthquake that you cried. It's not unheard of to cry when you're scared."

"I can't do it without touching my eyeball." She handed the drops back to Liv. "You do it for me."

After a few seconds, Liv said, "Good as new."

"Yeah, right."

"Let's go in."

But Jamie couldn't move. She was going to lose it again.

"Stop," Liv said. "Hold it together."

By the time they walked into the library's meeting room, Gigi was already sitting at the twenty-man table. Afon popped in a few seconds later. He came in not that long after them but still offered up an excuse.

"Had to batten down the hatches," he said. Obviously referring to the earthquake.

"We just got here too," Jamie said. And not in a nice way and with a tinge of damnation hanging in the air after her words.

When he sidled past Jamie, she caught notes of shampoo and laundry softener. He'd recently showered and slipped on freshly laundered clothing.

Afon ignored her and said, "Steph's not here?"

Liv answered, saying that she had texted her. "She says she won't be coming tonight or, for that matter, the next couple weeks. She didn't say why."

"Aw. And I was hoping we might," and here Afon bobbled his sandy eyebrows, "get together for a (wink, wink) drink after." He shifted his eyes to Jamie, who looked away from him. "Maybe *you* want to get a drink, tonight, James?"

She glared at him. "No, thank you," she said. "I need to get home. To Larry."

Liv coughed. Then covered her mouth.

"Sorry, it's a guy thing. We have to ask. It's in our DNA."

You had to give Afon that. He loved the ladies. Could the book club women really hate him? No. They could not. Still, at a room filled with female bodies drowning in estrogen and birth control pills, some thought he might tone down his maleness. They were used to Afon. Used to his guy ways. Plus, they were all women who had been married or were still married and who loved their men, well, most of them anyway. It wasn't like they weren't keen on the ways of men.

Jamie sat. She wasn't about to let Afon get to her tonight. She wouldn't give him the pleasure of looking at him. Instead, she scribbled something onto her notepad.

"Whatcha writing, Jamie? A note to Liv?" He chuckled.

"Grocery list, if you must know." Jamie often wrote lists during book club—to-do lists, grocery lists, wish lists.

"So, what happened with Steph?" Afon asked.

Liv's role was to head up the meetings. She ignored his question. "Let's get started. I have to leave a little early myself."

Everyone opened their copies of *Moon Spyer*, a novel by another local author.

Liv prompted the discussion. "Gigi, you start. What did you like about this story?"

Gigi talked for five minutes explaining how she enjoyed reading about the place where they all lived and that the landmarks in the novel were accurate. What she didn't like were the curse words and, "Why did she have to kill the little girl?"

"Gigi, she's not a real girl," Afon chimed in.

"Still, I don't like that part."

Liv cut in. "But it's the inciting event. The story revolves around the death of the little girl."

"Of course. This I realize. Still…" Gigi said.

"What about you, Jamie," Liv asked.

Did her nerves show? Were her hands shaking?

"Hmm," Jamie said, playing it cool using a reflective second before offering up an opinion. "I agree with Gigi about the setting. That was fun. But I don't agree about the death of the little girl. Although sad. The writer," everyone referred to all authors slated for the book club as *the writer*, "eased the information into the story slowly, bit by bit until the end when we fully see how the little sister's death touched everyone. I liked that." She paused, then added, "And her description. I like that too."

"Afon? Your turn."

"I liked the sex scenes."

Liv, Gigi and Jamie all groaned. Afon chuckled.

"I'm serious," he said. "The writer uses sex as a weapon."

"It's not *sex* when the act is not welcome, dear Afon," Gigi said, ever instructing.

"That's my point, Gigi. Call it rape if that suits you better. Label it. But it's more than rape. It's a tool people use to control others on the inside. Right? It's a power grab."

Everyone there nodded.

"My point. A weapon. And I liked it. I thought the writer handled each scene with finesse."

The women all seemed to breathe out at once.

Liv chimed in. "Here's what I thought. I thought the writer uses metaphor in a unique way so as to color the reader's opinion about certain aspects of the novel—the mother, the small town, drunk driving, many other elements. She also shows how lying and deceit can ruin people's lives."

She shot a look in Jamie's direction. Jamie looked down. It wasn't lost on Afon who followed the action. Gigi acted like she didn't notice.

"What just happened?" he said.

But Liv ignored him and continued, "I also enjoyed the slips into magical realism."

"Those were fun," Afon said. "Especially the Incredible Hulk one."

Gigi said, "That's because you're an incredible hulk."

"Ha. Ha," Afon responded. "Although, I am pretty fit, aren't I ladies?" He flexed a bicep.

"Okay!" Liv said, trying to reel in the discussion. "Now, what didn't we like."

"Marge," Gigi said.

"Hmm," Jamie said. "I sort of didn't like the way the *writer* made our town seem like it was set in some backwoods, *Deliverance* type of place. We're not Podunk."

"Yes, we are," Afon said. "Like," he took on a southern drawl, "My daddy said he *loves* me, know what I mean?"

"Oh bull," Jamie said. Her ire igniting immediately. "You're disgusting."

Gigi laughed then said, "I already told you...the little girl didn't have to die."

Liv rolled her eyes. "Okay, what next?"

Jamie said, "I'm not sure I will be around..."

Liv shook her head, stopping Jamie's next words.

"What?" Afon said. "What's going on between you two tonight?"

"I'm not sure, is all," Jamie said.

"What about *All the Light We Cannot See*?" Liv asked. "Haven't we all read that one?" Everyone nodded. "Then let's club it. Or *Crawdads*. We all read that one, right?" Again, all nods from everyone. "Which one, then?"

Afon chose *All the Light*. So, Jamie chose *Crawdads*. Gigi chose *Crawdads* too, and it was up to Liv to break the tie.

"That's why we need Steph here. If I choose *All the Light*, we have a tie. If *Crawdads*, Afon's gonna think we're teaming up on him. Aren't you, Af?"

"Don't you always?"

"Always," Liv said, but there was no humor in her voice.

Then Afon switched. "I don't mind if we read *Crawdads*. And by the way, where *is* Steph?"

Gigi began to fidget, then said, "Well, you didn't hear from me, but I heard she's having an affair with someone. I heard from a friend of Tom's who said Tom found out."

Jamie glared at Afon.

Afon shifted in his seat. "He found out?" he said.

Liv stopped it all by saying, "Oh good. We get to hear some good old-fashioned *Podunk*, backwoods, small town gossip. Just what I had hoped our meeting would devolve into." She stood and stormed out toward the bathrooms.

"What was *that* about?" Afon said.

"Don't take it wrong," Jamie said to Gigi. Then, she took off after Liv. "I'll find out."

CHAPTER 13
NOW—September 22, 2020

They're going to ask about the...identification.

I nearly decided not to go to book club. Liv had suggested as much.

Just slip on your jammies, Jamie. Relax. Pour a glass of wine. Curl up on the couch and watch a Law & Order rerun.

But I didn't.

It was thirty minutes before the meeting began. I had vacillated back and forth so long that I was only now preparing to leave the house.

It would be the first time back since Larry's *disappearance.* I indeed missed my friends and the meetings. It had been three months. More than a little trepidation filled me since it was on a previous book club evening that Larry went missing.

I miss you, Larry. So much. It hurts.

People around town called it "Larry's disappearance." Some said, "When Larry went missing." But the phrase *Larry's disappearance* was concise, easier to get out. And people always liked things better when they were easy. But a disappearance isn't easy. It was hard work. Many questions remained for authorities.

Why hadn't anyone seen him?

How far had he walked only to end up dead?

And the big question: Where was his body?

I was scrambling items together to take with me, like Liv's

novel, which we were book clubbing, and a notepad, my favorite, stuffing everything into a large tote bag, when I caught sight of my face in a mirror. I gasped and pulled out some lipstick from my bag. I needed color. I set my bag next to my jeans on the bed, which was still unmade since the morning, and ran into the bathroom. I dabbed on a thin layer of nude foundation around my eyes, rolled fawn-colored lipstick, and swiped mascara onto my lashes.

For years, my eyebrows had been speckled with gray, so as I swept a light whisk of brown onto my brows, someone knocked hard on my front door and my hand jerked. I had drawn an inverted V onto the top edge of my eyebrow, which created a questioning expression.

"Shit," I said. The inverted V also made me look like an angry emoticon. "Great," I said and tried to wipe the V away but ended up smearing it more. "Crap," I yelled down to whoever was at the door for them to wait.

I snagged the jeans from the bed. After rushing to get them on and zipped, I pulled on a heavy gray cardigan. Earlier, I'd left my shoes near the kitchen door where I needed them when I went outside.

As I rushed out of the bedroom over to the landing, I stumbled but caught myself on the railing stopping a nasty fall. My knees buckled and I slumped onto the landing to calm down.

I missed Larry so much. I just needed to sit for a spell.

But the person at the door knocked again.

"Just a minute!" I said. I was angry. I was scared. I was trying to rein in my emotions.

I had to get to the door. I had to scale the flight of stairs. My heart thumped. My stress soared.

For years, Larry and I raced up and down these stairs. Now, they seemed to warp in front of me like a wicked slide. Like a devil possessed them and was urging me forward to take a step. *Come on. Jump!* the devil said. *I'll catch you.* He winked.

After a few breaths, I stood again.

Through the door's window, I spotted a man. He was large and wearing a dark shirt and, from what I could tell through the fractured design of leaded glass, a pair of dark slacks. He cupped both hands onto the glass and was peering inside the house. His face darkened and splintered through the window. When he spotted me, he must have realized I was watching him and pulled back.

It irked me to think about him peering inside my house. Dammit. I needed a new door, a solid one, no windows.

"Just a sec!" I yelled. It came out rough. I didn't care. Who the hell thinks they can spy inside someone's home just because there's a window in the door? My cheeks flashed hot.

The time had to be close to the start of the meeting. I was going to be late if whoever this was didn't go away soon.

As I gripped the railing to head downstairs, steadying not only my wobbly legs but my wobbly mind, I managed to make my way down each of the fourteen stairs, albeit a little slower than normal.

From inside, I said, "Sorry. Just a second. I'm almost there."

However, as the gap shortened between me and the door, I could make out who the person was.

It was Rob.

A chill ran across my skin. I paused.

They always charge the spouse.

Before opening the door, I wiped sweat off my hands onto the hips of my jeans, then unlocked it and pulled it open.

"Oh, hey, Rob," I said. "I wasn't *expecting* you." The word expecting came out a higher pitch.

"Hey, Jamie. Sorry to pop by unannounced."

The slightest smile pulled against each corner of his lips. His pupils, so dark they seemed to float inside a pool of green irises. He placed both hands on both sides of the doorframe. If I needed to run, my only escape route would be to go under one of his arms.

I nudged the thought out of my brain. Why would I need to

escape? Rob is law enforcement. He's safe. Plus, I refuse to think of myself as a criminal. Larry's death (everyone suspecting him dead after three months) was not my fault. I did not *cause* it. But could I have prevented it? Only if I'd chained him to a chair. But guilt hunts you like an owl after a rat.

Rob was wearing his cop uniform, flak jacket and all. His belt still stocked with a baton, pepper spray, taser, and a handgun; the mic clipped to a shoulder strap as usual but was turned either off or down because it wasn't causing its usual static and chatter.

"Is everything okay?" I asked.

"Well, yeah. I just got off and wanted to check in on ya." With that he gave a full smile. "How you doin'?"

Was this a social call? Or was this San Juan County Sheriff's Office's standard operating procedure to check on a widow after taking her to the coroner's office to identify her husband's *foot*?

"As well as can be expected."

I drilled my eyes into his. He leaned back and glanced out onto the porch. I couldn't believe he had neglected to tell me that the identification would not only be Larry's tennis shoe but also his foot.

Stating the obvious, he said, "It wasn't easy."

"No, Rob. It wasn't. Not only was it *not* easy, it was *horrifying*."

He pulled away, unlocking his hands from the door frame, and crossed his arms. He shifted his weight back and forth. His jaw twitched. He turned away from me and bent slightly to look up to the sky.

Night would officially fall within two hours. It would be dusk by the time the meeting ended and dark by the time I walked back inside the house, assuming everyone was going to hang a few minutes at the library afterward.

What was he looking at?

"Rob," I said, hoping to shake his attention back.

"The moon's waxing crescent," he said. His eyes still lifted upward, and he thumbed behind his head toward where I stood. "Out east, out there the moon is on the rise."

And although we couldn't see the east side of the island from the front porch, he added, "It's pretty." Then as though he were speaking to the moon, the sky, and the setting sun, he said, "I have some news. I bought a bigger house. Not far from town but not so close as my old place. You know, and, well, I got a bottle of champagne in my car and was thinking if you weren't…"

I'd been asked on dates before and this sounded remarkably close. I stopped him.

"Oh, Rob. Gosh, I hate to say this. I mean. Congratulations on the new house but I have a meeting tonight."

He nodded as though he already knew I would say no.

He said, "Book club?"

He turned to face me again and when he did, he shoved his hands deep into his pockets, slightly lifting his shoulders. Him standing there like that reminded me of an embarrassed school-boy. I was surprised he remembered the evenings of our meetings.

"Well, yes," I said. I furrowed my eyebrows. "It will be the first time since, well, since…you know."

"I do."

But how could he?

"You *do*?"

The question brought a gush of rose into his cheeks.

"Library's on my evening route. I check for your car each time I pass. But I was off early today. Swapped for someone so I could close on the house. And to celebrate." Before he let me say anything, deny him again, he said, "It's good to hear you're reclaiming your old ways."

"Reclaiming my *old* ways? Are you saying I'm *old*, Rob?" I was trying to make light of my rejection, trying to make a joke. But it was a lame one and either he didn't get it or felt embarrassed by his choice of words because he scrabbled around for a better descriptor to recover from his previous word choice.

"Not you," he said. "I mean. You're not old. Anything but...aw, geez, Jamie. I think you're amazing. You know what I mean. Getting back to your *routines*. Your previous *habits*."

"Aw. My *habits*. Well, if I don't get going, Rob, I'll be late for *this* habit. But was there something you needed me for, from me? I mean, you know. Regarding Larry?"

"Yeah, I do," he said. He squinted hard at me. "But maybe another time," he said. "I wasn't sure if you were going to go, you know, after three months not going, and if you weren't, then we coulda talked. But since you're going, I'll let you go."

He'll let me go.

But Rob didn't leave right away and kept his hands deep in his pockets. Then, he turned and hopped down the rock stairs. Again, the way he did made him look more boyish than official.

I felt bad for rushing him away.

"Definitely another time," I said. His back was still to me. "Want to talk tomorrow?"

He didn't say anything. Instead, he raised his right hand without looking back and got into his cop car. I waved, trying to get his attention, but he didn't (or wouldn't) look my way.

So, I waited until he drove out of sight before going inside. Did it look wrong to show up at the book club? Was it too early to socialize—after only three months? Did Rob think badly of me? Was it too soon?

As I closed the door, I heard his car revving as he drove down our road in the direction of town.

I rubbed my hands over my arms to stop my skin from prickling. It was off: his impromptu appearance, my rejection, his awkwardness.

And what had he wanted to talk to me about? Was it about his new place? Or was it something about Larry's case?

Questions raced in me. Did they find out something more?

I couldn't stop wondering what he wanted to tell me.

CHAPTER 14
NOW—September 22, 2020

I snuck a peek at the timestamp on my cellphone.

It took only two minutes. Only two minutes before they started in with their stupid questions.

Of course, it did.

Afon started in first. "Was it his foot?" A smirk formed around each word.

I hated the way Randie had pulled the flaps open to reveal what was inside the shoe. I hated the smell. The putrid burst of rancid meat rising from the shoe, the mix of seawater and human decay, made me want to run. I hated the way I became nauseated and covered my mouth; appalled by the sight of Larry's rotting foot.

I twisted a lock of hair to my nose. The scent of rose shampoo lingered within the strands but wasn't exactly fresh. I wished I hadn't decided to forego a shower this morning when I decided I didn't have time.

I was lost in a shower I hadn't taken, the fading rose of my hair, and the smell from Larry's cadaverous foot.

"James?" Afon said again. "Was that too insensitive?" He enjoyed this strange goading technique.

Liv sat back hard in her chair. "Jesus, Af," she said.

My eyes flashed at her. For whatever reason, I didn't mind when people used the F-word. Hell, I even used it on occasion.

But I hated when people used God's or Jesus' name as a curse. Liv knew it.

The nauseating scent of Afon's cologne burst back to the forefront of my ire. I unwound the cord of my hair.

Everyone was staring. The stark fluorescent lights pasting everyone's skin in an unnatural tone.

They all look dead.

Then, I must look dead too.

Afon's death mask broke into life. He was chewing his gum. Giving it hell. Smacking and popping the wad in his mouth. Irritating me to no flipping end. What seemed worse was he knew, and he seemed to be enjoying using a wad of his slimy gum to underline his gloating face *and* his stupid question.

I felt my eyes tighten. I embraced the irritation.

And I was going to say, *Will you take that God-blessed gum out of your mouth you disgusting pig*? But he seemed to intuit the coming response. He reached for a napkin, spat out the gum, wadded it into the napkin, and lobbed it like a basketball at the metal wastebasket.

It missed.

I smiled.

But then Afon popped up from his chair and arched his back, stretching it. At the same time, he seemed to flex his muscles all at once. I wanted to yack into the same wastebasket Afon tried to throw his napkin into.

After he performed this little show, I realized he'd probably missed the shot intentionally so that he could prance around to show off his physique.

"Afon," Liv said. "Can you please pull it together?" She looked exhausted. I hadn't ever seen Liv this pale, even under the hideous library lights. "I'm still hoping to get some good feedback from you guys on my story."

"Sorry, Liv. Of course, dear." On his way back to his chair, he glided his hand across her shoulder blades. She leaned nearer to the table trying to escape his touch.

Gigi picked one chip from the bowl sitting on the table. My stomach growled. I had fully intended to grab a handful of something to snack on in the car but after Rob's sudden appearance, grabbing some food slipped my mind.

A plate of green grapes sat wet on another plate next to the chips. I reached for them. Gigi slid the food closer making it easier for me. She slid the chips after then grabbed a paper plate and a napkin for me. I gave her a weak grin.

Afon hadn't yet taken a seat. His hands gripped the metal frame of his chair, and he was leaning in over it.

"Well," he said, "was it?" He wasn't about to drop the subject of Larry's foot. "I'm a surgeon. Don't fault me if I want to know details. It's what I do."

Please, let it go, Afon.

Liv jumped on him. "Good lord, Afon. How freaking insensitive can you be? Even if you're a doctor. What the hell's wrong with you?" She wasn't about to take any of his crap tonight. In fact, she raised her voice—a very non-Liv thing to do. "Drop it. Okay!?" she said. "Anyway, it's what you *did*. Past tense, Af."

I smiled but only at my plate of grapes and chips. I felt a good amount of satisfaction from Liv's protection.

And for the first time I'd known him, he apologized, albeit in his very Afon way.

"Well, it's not the first time someone's said something like this to me."

He actually appeared sorry.

"James? Are you okay?" Liv said.

Leave it to Liv to mitigate Afon's glaring lack of diplomacy.

But to appease Afon's curiosity and his sideways apology, I said, "I wasn't okay yesterday. I'm just *trying* not to think about it." But I couldn't help shooting him a glare. "Okay, *Afon*?"

He sat and leaned back. He folded his arms, pressing his fists under his biceps to enhance their size. Afon was a child. And

this is the thing: He wasn't unattractive. He just spoke and acted in unattractive ways. It was as though his being a surgeon,
having all that money, gave him a sense of entitlement. That,
because of it, he somehow earned the right to be an insensitive
prick. To treat people as subject matter rather than sentient be-
ings.

"Look," he said, "purely scientific interest, *James.*"

He attempted to soften the blow. His bedside manner must
have been excellent. Not because he was caring. Far from it. But
because he was *manipulative.*

Then Gigi chimed in. Using her most diplomatic Gigi-*isms*,
she said. "Jamie, we all know this is difficult to talk about. And
if you don't want to, we *all* understand. But did you make an
identification?" The uppermost layer of the questioning sounded sincere but if you knew Gigi, if you dug down, you knew she
used diplomacy to weasel out answers. That any answer you
gave would end up a punchline for the next *upper-crust-only-
get-together*—another party I wouldn't be invited to. And for
once, I was happy for it.

That was the moment I realized Gigi was a gossip. That all
those times she'd confided in me about juicy scandals around
the island, always demanding complete confidence, a confidence
I always gave, thinking she was only telling me tales about others. But to suddenly realize she might also be spreading tales
about *me*?

It's one thing to be a recipient of gossipy news and quite another to be the subject of gossipy news. I knew Gigi would take
whatever I said at this moment and gossip about me too. I felt
duped.

And yet, in a way I also felt relieved, happy. Happy that I finally recognized Gigi for who she really was. A fake and a pho-
ny. That she would take something as intimate and tender as
Larry and my situation, his disappearance and now the foot,
and she would let it out of this room and whisper and buzz
about the situation. It hurt.

I envisioned it all playing out: all the wealthiest people there in their most fashionable attire, people I knew mostly from the sidelines, all gathering around Gigi to hear her relay that "Yes! It was Larry's, and yes, his foot was still inside the shoe!"

As soon as I got home that night, I was going to rummage through my box of sentimentalities and burn all her sympathy cards! What a fool I was.

Afon smiled. He lifted his hands in Gigi's direction. Like, *See? We all want to know.*

Liv rubbed the skin under her eye. She shook her head. It wasn't just me, Afon got under Liv's skin too. He was a chigger, a niggling insect.

Honestly, I became hyper-sensitive about everything Afon said or did since the *running incident.* I never told a soul but couldn't be sure Afon hadn't. Afon gave our *chance* encounter a fair amount of planning before it happened.

He appeared one morning out of nowhere. I typically started running from off the front door and headed out of our driveway. It's an uninterrupted, six-mile run in one big circle back to the porch.

Not long after my start that day, I was surprised to see the figure of a man rounding the corner about a hundred yards ahead of me. It was Afon. He acted as though it was a surprise for him as well.

"James! I didn't realize you ran out here." His words jumped around, coming out breathy from running in place in front of me. "Isn't this a happy coincidence," he said.

The term *coincidence* caused my hair to stand on end. I should've listened to my body's reaction. But I shrugged it off. Thought the hair of my neck had prickled because of the morning chill. It couldn't be anything more underhanded, or could it?

Was Afon trying too hard to look nonchalant?

He told me he wanted to show me something. Something in the woods he'd seen. A fawn, he'd said, it might be injured.

My affection for deer was well known around the island.

101

People knew we fed a small herd daily. He added that it might be one of the fawns I was feeding.

It was unconscionable to think a fawn wouldn't hear our feet tramping through the woods or Afon calling me deeper into the woods, away from the road.

I couldn't pinpoint the moment his suggestion to go into the woods with him sounded like a good idea. It was the mention of the fawn, right? Had to be. Because I didn't want to fool around on Larry with Afon. Did I? And when did I even consider the possibility of an affair at all? Was Larry's dementia turning me away from him?

Sex with Afon wouldn't be anything but the base act itself. He fooled around with everyone. So, why would I be any different to Afon? He'd have his one-off with me and done. Like a dirty sock.

Had I back then considered the possibility of sneaking down my running pants, grabbing the trunk of the tree, and letting him have a go at me?

And there he was now across the table from me with that tell-tale smirk.

What strikes me most about the woods was his quickening breath in gulps as he closed in on me and how his hands shook.

So, I stared that glib face of his down and squinted.

I said, "What if I told everyone here tonight that it *wasn't* Larry's shoe? Hmm? What then?"

Of course, I was toying with them now. Mostly for the benefit of Afon.

I glanced over at Liv. My face glowing from screwing with them all. Glowing brighter than the rest under these hideous lights.

But Liv wasn't smiling. She closed her eyes and dropped her head.

Had I pissed her off? Because now she looked concerned or worried, even angry. And maybe all those emotions together.

I clutched my hands together on top of the table, a schoolgirl being hushed by the homeroom teacher.

Liv coiled her hair then tucked it up inside a tangle of hair. In the process, she took on a new demeanor. She looked cooler. Her expression changed. Her frown left. A look, strange and difficult to pinpoint, filled her eyes. A look of superiority, a stoic and judging mien took over. She sat up straight.

But maybe I was being too sensitive? Lately I was sensing an otherness in her—maybe from what had happened between us three months before. Something Liv and I swore we would never tell anyone else.

I'm only trying to help you, she'd said.

I was inconsolable.

Liv held me. We went too far. Made a decision that would change our friendship forever.

Had Liv told anyone else? Had she told Paul, her *husband*? Would she *betray* me that way?

What I saw at the morgue was none of anyone else's business. Saying anything about it would only send off a wildfire blazing through the island's grapevine. Afon and the rest could all go fly a *flipping* kite. The people who needed to know, knew.

I was sure word would sift out from the coroner's office soon enough. I wasn't going to fulfill their curiosities by telling them myself. To endure their sad looks. Their sad and fake expressions.

And yes. Yes, dammit! It was Larry's shoe. However, the most heartbreaking part was a little part of Larry was still inside his shoe.

CHAPTER 15
NOW—September 22, 2020

After refusing to say another word about what I witnessed at the coroner's office, things at the meeting went somewhat back to normal.

"Liv," Afon asked, "how is it we have nothing on you?"

"I write enough about this place that I know what *not* to do." Her grin let everyone know, me especially, that she was drawing from biblical scripture. She knew the Bible. Well, in fact. She just didn't believe any longer. A disbelief she said that had developed over many years. She finally kicked faith to the curb. In fact, it was only a few months ago when she up and quit believing.

Since then, we had tons of conversations about faith and God. But we agreed to disagree so our friendship wouldn't suffer. Liv acted in faith, spoke in faith. She just said she didn't *have* faith.

"Someone *must* know something juicy about you," Afon continued. He was still haranguing Liv.

"They might *think* they have something juicy on me, Af," she said. "But you gotta find the bodies first." A quick glance my way. No smile.

Afon glanced my way too. "Okay," he said. "What happened there?"

Liv said, "I'm sure I don't know what you're talking about."

"You two. That look."

"I can't look at my friend now?"

"James? What's up?"

I fidgeted with my pen then wrote down *sanitary wipes* on a fresh grocery list.

Gigi sighed, and when she did, Afon set his sights on her. But Gigi shrugged him off and said, "Please don't bring me into this. I've been here long enough to have made more than a few faux pas and a stack of skeletons."

"Do tell!" Afon said, turning up his charm meter to high mode. He shifted in his seat and faced Gigi.

"Afon." She sounded as though she were going to dismiss him and not answer. She blew out a quick puff of air—her typical Gigi dismissal. Then, she smiled. She got this look, like a child who had found a secret door inside a secret closet, and she changed her mind midstream. I glanced over to Liv. She set her chin into her hand to listen, but she wasn't amused. She appeared irritated.

"Go ahead," I said. "Tell us another Gigi story." Gigi loved to talk about herself.

"Okay. But you better take it to the grave." She squinted in a fake-serious way, then she added, "It wasn't even a year since William died."

"Your husband," Afon inserted.

"Yes, of course, Afon. My husband." She rolled her eyes. "It was nothing really." A premise she hoped we would buy into which didn't work. But by now, even Liv was hooked.

"A *man*," she said, adding emphasis, "who will remain *nameless*." She shot a maternal look at Afon—a preemptive strike for him to dare think about asking—and continued. "Asked me to dinner at Vinny's."

"I'm calling Jules! He'll tell me," Afon said. Joy danced in his eyes.

"He's been sworn to secrecy," she said. "And he wouldn't tell you anything. He doesn't like you very much."

"Their scallopine sucks," Afon said.

"Yes, well, you should keep certain things to yourself." Then, Gigi continued. "So, the dinner was pleasant, but I didn't realize it was a date until he ordered dessert for us, which I kind of discounted until he asked if I wanted to follow him home. Can you *believe* that?" Her voice pitched high, and she laughed. "I mean, come on, it had been only seven months and I wasn't *nearly* ready to date. I never thought I would again. Plus, who wants to drive from town to Roche Harbor and back in the dark?"

"Aha!" Afon said, "Roche Harbor, you say?" He scratched something invisible under his nose. "Here's my take."

"Oh Afon, please," Gigi said.

"No, let me fill in some blank spots." He cleared his throat. A typical Afon thing to do as if figuring a probable diagnosis to a puzzling illness. "We know, don't we, gals, that Gigi isn't going to go out with just anyone. She would never, and I mean never, go out even on a non-date with a man who didn't have means. Gigi likes only to be seen with wealthy people, like *moi*. You see, we tend to date within our own tax bracket. It's a risk-free thing to do. People within similar tax brackets don't lose nearly as much as when we *slide* to a lower rung."

I said, "You mean, tax bracket." I was squinting at him.

"Yes, James, a lower rung tax bracket. Why? What did you think I meant?"

I shook my head, crossed my arms, and sat back in my chair.

So, he continued his theory. "Lawsuits, you know? Marriage. Ho boy! If we marry lower, we suffer greater losses. Even with prenuptials which tend to have term limits—say, ten years and the contract fizzles to nothing. And boom. She leaves with half of everything." He was gesturing and shifting in his seat as he spoke, putting on a one-man show.

"God, Afon. You're a pig," Liv said, finally taking all she could take.

"Pig is the nicest thing you could say about him, Liv," I said.

But Afon didn't stop. He went on. "Wait. Wait. Here's another clue. Dessert, she said, right? Desserts are a date night...affair...for lack of a better word." He laughed at his joke. Gigi folded her arms in front of her but then brought them back down and straightened the wrinkles she'd created in her cashmere sweater. "Dessert," he said, "implies...how shall I say...deee*sert*! If you catch my drift." He made those stupid bobbly eyes again. "So, Gigi." He turned to face her directly now. "At some point, you must've been enjoying your *date* enough to consider furthering it into a more intimate setting. Why else would Mr. Mystery Man ask you back to his place?"

"You're deplorable," she said.

He pounded the tabletop. "Drumroll please! The *last* clue, of course, is *the* most telling. The most obvious. He lives in Roche Harbor, again, a place where those with means band together. I know who it is. Does anyone else?" He scanned Liv's face then mine. "Okay, then. If no one else wants to play, I'll tell you. It's..." Again, with the drumroll...

"Afon! Stop!" Gigi shouted.

My heart ground to a halt.

Liv's chest heaved filling with air.

Afon laughed. "Oh Gigi, I have no idea who the guy is. I'm just messing with you, dear." He continued to laugh.

And we all jumped—as they say—out of our skin when the door flew open.

CHAPTER 16
NOW—September 22, 2020

Steph slinked in. Trying not to interrupt, she hunched as she crept to the empty seat across from me with a chair between her and Afon. She looked like she'd just stepped out of the spa—fresh and rosy, hair perfect, makeup to match (in fact too much makeup for our meetings), nails freshly polished, killer outfit. She placed Liv's latest novel on the table in front of her and patted it once.

She mouthed the word *sorry* to everyone. And when she positioned her tiny butt in the exact spot on the chair that she wanted, I saw it when she looked up at me. Liv did too. Gigi couldn't because she didn't have a face-forward view of her and neither did Afon.

When our eyes connected, I acted like I wasn't staring at the bruise under her left eye. There had been rumors about their marriage. Still…

I placed my hands in my lap to hide a chipped thumbnail I'd been digging at.

"We thought you were going to miss," Liv said.

"Things changed," she said. She adjusted herself in her seat and shot a smile, nodding toward Afon but not looking at him directly.

"Steph," he said. "Makes my day." He reached across the chair between them and patted her hands which she had folded in front of her.

She gave an awkward smile and swiped hair behind her ears. "Sorry to interrupt. What was everyone talking about? Please. Go on."

"Nothing," I said.

But Afon wasn't going to let it die. He had zero clue and zero boundaries.

"Actually, Steph, my dear," he said. "Gigi was telling us all about a date she had seven months after William died."

Steph gasped.

"Yep," he said. "Seems the timing was off or else she may have gone the Full Monty with him."

"Afon, please," Gigi said.

"Really?" Steph shot a surprised glance to Gigi. "Do I know him?"

But Gigi put a hand over her mouth when she caught sight of Steph's bruised eye.

Steph turned and faced me. Our eyes locked together.

Again, Afon was clueless and had missed all the interaction between the women in the room.

"That's the thing, Steph. She's refusing to out him," he said.

"Afon." My voice was charged with anger and confusion. "Can we *please* get back to Liv's book?"

"I didn't realize we'd started," Liv said.

Steph sat back, pointed at Liv's book, and said, "It's good, Liv." As if the word *good* was compliment enough.

Liv tightened her lips. She followed with her usual, "*Why* is it good, Steph?" Liv loathed phrases like *it was good* or *it's okay* or *I didn't like it*. She wanted to know why. Why is it good? Why is it just okay? Or *why* didn't someone like it? But that was Liv. Always needing details, the minutia of why.

She'd often say, "Story is in the details." Telling us that story can be found in the smallest bit of information; in words an author chooses to insert that can become the most important bit of material in the end.

"Why are you like this?" Steph asked. "Why can't you just take thumbs-up or down?" She pushed her chair back. "I don't know why I came. Maybe I should just go."

"No!" Afon grabbed her shoulder when she shifted in her seat, pressing her down.

"Afon, stop." She moved out from under his grip.

She scanned our faces, mine and Liv's, before settling on Liv.

"This book club, right?" Liv said. "If we're not going to *discuss* books, then why am I wasting my time?" But before anyone could respond, she said, "Because it's important to me *why* you like or don't like a book. It's important to authors. We care at readings and signings but mostly, here, at book clubs, where we are actually supposed to be discussing plot and character, theme and tone, what connects with the reader and what doesn't." And here's where Liv sort of lost it. "I expect *more* from all of you!"

Steph glared at Liv and said, "Well, that's *your* problem. We all want what we want from these *little* meetings."

Liv glared at Steph. The response she had building inside her was being written across her face.

"Here we go," Gigi muttered, crossing her arms; this time not caring about the cashmere.

"No, Gigi," Afon interjected, "you're not getting off that easy. Fess up. Who's the beau?"

Gigi, Liv, and I all said in unison, "Shut up, Afon."

I chuckled but drew a critical look from Steph. "Don't say that to him," she said.

My mouth fell open. I nearly told her to eff-off but didn't.

"Are you kidding me? Give me a break," I said.

No wonder Tom socked her. I wanted to. Part of me commiserated with him having to live with her, the little snit. She deserved a good backhand. If I could've reached across right then, I would have...

Black eye or not.

CHAPTER 17
NOW—September 22, 2020

The earth is spinning faster and I'm losing my balance.

I stood up and leaned across the table at Steph. Our eyes locked until Afon broke the silence.

"We need to finish this," he said.

I stacked my belongings into my arms. "It's finished for me."

But he didn't drop it. "Come on, James. Book club's not over." His voice took on a whiny tone.

"Like I said, I'm done." I squinted at Afon, then said, "You don't know, do you?"

A confused expression and then he shook his head.

"You both think no one knows about your little," my hand danced between them, *"nuptials,"* I said.

Gigi gasped like it was the first time she'd heard about their affair. The fake.

Afon's and Steph's eyes connected. Steph's were sheepish, with a hint of apology. Afon reached to her face.

"Your eye," he said.

Steph pulled back. "Stop," she said.

Their entire interaction gave them up.

"Right before I had to take his car keys. That's when it happened. Am I right?" I asked her.

Steph tried to hush me. I cut her off.

"Right around the same time you two began your little fling

with *Afon*. I think that's important to know. Don't you, Afon?" He played with something on his pant leg and tried to be invisible.

Liv and Gigi lay low, out of the line of fire.

"Miss Perfect, here. With her prim and proper hair and makeup can't seem to keep her legs closed for a second if someone gives her a hint of interest."

I slammed down my things and leaned both hands onto the table.

"We used to call girls like you in high school Jiffy. Like the peanut butter? Spreads easy, you know?"

Her beige makeup couldn't hide the blush rising into her skin. She dropped her stare and checked everyone else's face. Gigi wouldn't look at her. Instead, she interlaced her fingers then rubbed her thumbs against each other. Liv sat back and crossed her arms. Afon refused to lower his hand from over his right eye and focused on his lap.

It felt good to finally see them both in their places; it felt like justice.

Running around. Hiding what everyone knew they were doing. They were Adam and Eve, naked in the garden, eating a forbidden apple. And once exposed, they were ashamed.

"So, yes. Everyone in flipping town knows. Even law enforcement."

Steph's face shot up to meet mine.

"That's right," I said. "I had to tell them because I needed their help. I mean, if Larry got away from the house without me knowing..." I let my voice trail off. "It's a twenty-four-hour-a-day job, taking care of a man with dementia."

With my final words, my body weakened. And I had to sit.

Steph took in a deep breath of air and spoke, "Well, what about you and Afon?"

From the corner of my eye, I saw Liv shoot a look at me. I ignored Liv and set my sights on Afon. "You told her?"

He wanted to crawl inside of his own skin.

"Do you want *me* to tell her what really happened? 'Cause I have my own special take on it, Afon."

He grumbled something inaudible.

"We couldn't hear you," I said. "Please, Afon. Please say it again." He knew I wasn't fooling around and that he was going to have to tell the truth.

He said, "I *said*, nothing happened."

Steph continued to avoid eye contact with anyone.

"You said you did it in the woods." Her voice was shrill and fearful.

"Afon..." I said, urging him to explain.

"I told Jamie there was a fawn and that I thought it was injured."

"Was there?" she asked.

I couldn't believe her question.

"It was a ploy, Steph."

Liv folded her arms and at the head of the table to Gigi was shaking her head and looked like she was about to faint.

Steph glared at Afon. But Afon had gone mute.

"There was no fawn," I said.

Her eyes widened and she looked lost in thought while she searched for something in her memory.

Finally, she said, "So, what happened when you found no fawn?"

"Steph, nothing happened except him trying to grope me. I flew out of the woods and ran home."

Her tone took on a defensive quality. "Well, if that's true, why were you running with him?"

"Afon..." Again, allowing him to answer. "Want to explain to her what happened? For real this time?"

He shook his head, then slowly looked up into Steph's eyes, which had turned veiny. "I knew where she ran, Steph. Everyone knows she runs that circle."

"I didn't," she said.

"Well, I do," I said. "Most mornings. I'm out my drive by

seven and back home by eight fifteen. Clockwork."

"Well, that doesn't mean Afon..."

Afon cut her off. "Good lord, Steph. I used to park my car at the end of the road and act like I just happened to be there. Okay? You need me to spoon-feed it to you?"

Liv raised a hand to her mouth. I couldn't tell from her expression if she wanted to laugh or cry.

Again, I gathered my things up. "Well, this has been a freaking load of fun," I said. "I think I might have to miss next time."

I pulled my purse over my shoulder and slipped out the side door.

CHAPTER 18
NOW—September 22, 2020

Through sickness and health. Till death do us part.

I was outside, free of them. Free of them all.

But my legs became concrete. I couldn't leave. Not that way. Not with them making up stories behind my back. I wanted the truth out. So, I turned back. Would I turn to salt?

I flew open the door. Everyone flinched and turned my way.

"I'm not leaving just yet," I said. "Not before I tell everyone what happened with Larry not long after he was diagnosed with dementia." I glared into Steph's bruised eye and hoped my words would bruise the other one. "Because as you know, Steph, the truth will set you free."

A wicked smile crossed my lips.

"You snobby little bitch," she said. "I don't care if Larry is missing or dead or whatever. You have no right to talk about me. I don't give a shit what you're going through." She pressed back in her chair, her face blotching with anger, her eyes watery.

The room sounded hollow while everyone figured out what to do or say next.

But I spoke first, "No, you're right, Steph. I have no right to talk to you that way about something as trivial as the truth." I paused. "But Steph. While I stood by my husband at the worst of times, what did you do?" No one in the room took a breath.

"That's right. It's not a rumor. She *slept* with Larry. And yet I still stayed with him to the bitter end. But you? You pop from one bed to the next. Right Afon?" I set my ire on him. My face warped under my anger. "One bed. To. The. Next." I dragged my attention away from Afon and back to Steph. "You think Tom didn't know? Doesn't know? Then you're the fool, not him. He finally had enough and look what you have to show for it. An ugly, shining bruise."

Steph smirked, then said, "Well, Larry sure didn't seem to mind." Her face still red but now resolved.

"He had *dementia*. You took advantage of a man with dementia. What sort of sick freak does something like that?" I paused and went on. "Know how I found out? He told me. He laughed because he couldn't tell right from wrong. He apologized but he was never to blame. You were. He never deserved getting this disease. You know, Steph, you should go to work at a convalescent center because then you'd have your pick of all the mindless men you could ever dream of."

Afon's chair creaked when he leaned back.

Steph didn't defend herself. No one wanted to say anything.

Afon dared a peek over the table at Liv. Liv turned from him across the table to Steph who went silent, stunned. Finally, Afon turned to Gigi who looked up at me.

After a few beats, Afon said, "I brought a flask of whiskey."

Gigi chuckled nervously then let out what sounded like a gallon of air.

I realized I was holding my breath too.

"Holy crap," Liv said. "And I thought tonight was going to be just a run of the mill meeting."

Afon pulled a flask out of his back pocket. He stood and handed it to me. I took a swig. The alcohol burned and sucked my breath away. And yet, I finally felt like I could breathe again. I relayed the flask across the table to Liv, who took a swig. She leaned across the table and tried to hand it to Gigi, who shook her head, so Liv handed it to Steph instead who took one dainty sip.

"I want another," I said.

Afon took it from Steph and handed it again to me. The liquor felt warmer the second time but not so sharp against my throat, so I took another longer sip.

"Hey. Come on," Afon said. He opened his palm. I relinquished the container back to him. He took two short swigs then pocketed the flask back into his jeans.

"Okay," he said, "now that that's over..." and his words fizzled into the ozone. "Liv, your book was *good*."

Although the evening ended much lighter than it had devolved into, this time when I walked out of the meeting room and into the dark night, I knew it would be my last.

But then Liv swung open the door and followed me.

CHAPTER 19
NOW—September 22, 2020

"Are you okay?" I asked. We were whispering.

"I'm fine. I just needed to talk to you. The question is: are *you* okay?" Liv said.

I leaned against the library's board-and-batten wall. "It was Larry's shoe, Liv."

All the freckles in her face seemed to vanish. "Was his…"

"Ohmygod," I said.

I covered my mouth to stifle any sound. But then I pulled myself together. I couldn't have anyone see me so unraveled. They would ask questions, questions that I didn't have answers to. At least, no answers I wanted to reveal.

I said, "I have to tell you something."

Liv nodded and folded her arms. Her eyes moist, glistening under an obscurity of nightfall.

"I can't wrap my head around it. I mean, well, maybe a fox or raccoon…"

"What? What are you talking about?" She was getting impatient for the information.

"Okay. Answer this. The shoelace, Liv. Did you notice if he was wearing shoelaces?"

She leaned next to me against the wall. "God. I don't." She raised both hands to her mouth, her fingers dancing over her lips. "Oh man. I don't remember. I was so grossed out. I'm sorry, James. I just, I think I blocked a lot of it out."

"Liv, I'm one hundred percent sure he was. I can't scrub the scene out of my head and every single time, his shoe had shoelaces."

"Okay. So what? why is that important?"

"It's important because the shoelaces weren't there when I identified him yesterday."

I waited for that to sink in. She pushed off the wall and got in my face.

"Oh, man. Jamie."

"Shh, keep your voice down."

"You're freaking me out."

"*I'm* freaking *you* out? What are all their looks for? What was all that about in there? I know they can tell."

Jamie recalled embracing Larry, pressed against chest, his heart on autopilot from the tick-tick of his mechanical heart valve.

Tick-tick, tick-tick.

"They can't tell anything other than something's going on with us."

Liv's eyes flared, a feral cat caught in a net, wild and dangerous. And I wondered if Liv was seeing the same thing in her own eyes?

She pivoted as though leaving, going back inside the library. But then she stopped when I said, "I don't know what to do."

Liv pulled me into an embrace, but I shrank away.

"What the hell? What if someone sees?"

Liv stepped back but kept a hand on my arm. The feral cat had morphed into a mother bear—protective, caring, but still dangerous. Liv tipped her head then pulled me, egging me closer until finally we were willingly holding each other.

"Why did you come by, Liv? What made you come by that day? Why can't you just leave me alone? I can take the fall. No one needs to know you were there at all."

"You don't know, Jamie?" She pulled back so we were face

to face. "I love you. That's why." And tenderly, she kissed my cheek. Then, she said, "Either come in or leave but if I don't get back in there, they're really going to get suspicious."

I shook my head that I wasn't going inside, and we pulled out of the embrace until only our fingertips were touching and then I turned and walked away.

CHAPTER 20
THEN—June 20, 2020

We have so little time. The world is breaking apart. Or are these memories all part of a dream?

Jamie ran through the scenario again making sure she didn't forget anything.

First, she got the emergency notification via cell phone alert system—an earthquake, a real rumbler, rolled under the island at 6.7 magnitude. Another alert followed explaining how to prevent damage to homes—turn off gas lines at the source, check for pipe breakages in water lines, check water levels often, they provided an emergency number with a recorded message and, finally, a website resource reiterating steps to take before, during and after a big earthquake.

All morning, Larry had been ranting again about her trying to kill him. He often had bouts of confusion and agitation since the dementia had worsened. He'd followed her out of the master bathroom yelling, through the bedroom haranguing her, his body intruding and angry. He finally stopped assailing her at the top of the landing where he pinned her against the guest room door. A spot so close to the stairwell it made the interaction precarious and frightening.

And something she needed to remember if asked: Twice, she'd fallen from the very spot where he had her pinned. Fortunately, she'd only come out with a few nasty bruises and scrapes on one hip, her legs, and arms. She once twisted her shoulder trying to avoid a fall. She'd broken no bones but limped around for days. Each time it seemed a miracle that she hadn't killed herself by breaking her neck.

Jamie also remembered how she quailed under Larry's yelling. She was smashed against a French door.

Looking back, it was as though God was watching because He gave her an out.

The lights flickered. Screeching as loud as a train filled every atom inside and outside the house. The earth groaned and the house shook.

She felt drunk. Couldn't keep her balance.

Larry too. His arms flailed up and down. Then, he stumbled. He grappled for her but far too late because he fell sideways, then backwards, nearer the first step down.

He was a clown in clown shoes slip-sliding on a banana peel. Waa, waa, waa! When his feet slipped out from under him. He flailed again. He tried to grab hold of her, of anything near him, trying to catch his balance.

And that shoe. That big clown shoe so close to the edge...

...slid off the top of the landing...

...and Larry stumbled out of sight.

One second, he was there. The next, he was gone.

BRAIN INJURY—Then & Now

CHAPTER 21

On the third day of Larry's disappearance, Liv and Jamie stood several yards outside the cordoned off area. CSI and S&R agents roped off the gaping hole. They'd taped strands of yellow crime scene tape around a series of tree trunks forming an enormous, abstract circle sectioning off a good acre area around the crevice, the dark, bottomless chasm.

The crevice appeared like a dead ogre with its mouth gaping open, its jagged lips rotting and sour, decomposing around the edges.

Liv and Jamie stood shoulder to shoulder both wrapping their arms around their waists as if it were cold outside. But the day was anything but cold. The temp hovered in the mid-seventies although the wind *was* picking up. In fact, weather reports expected gusts to crank up to thirty knots, nearly thirty-five miles per hour. The NOAA posted an online wind advisory warning small boats about the treachery of high waves and dangerous water conditions and how waves only ten feet high could capsize smaller boats.

Jamie's hair fluttered around her face. Liv had pulled hers into her standard ponytail, which whipped like a horse's tail swatting at flies.

Chewing on a thumbnail, Jamie sensed people fixating on her rather than the hole. Rob had one hand over his mouth.

Is he smiling?

And what did her own face admit to him?

Then, she thought, he winked. Did he? Surely not. If he had, he covered for it by rubbing one finger into his eye socket.

Or maybe he *did* get a fleck of something in his eye. With the wind and all...

Then the earth growled.

Larry adjusted his footing.

Another earthquake?

But no one else seemed to feel the ground shift.

Then Rob gave a final quick glance over to Jamie.

"Liv," she whispered. "Did you feel that?"

But Liv shook Jamie off and hushed her but seemed to pull in closer. Or maybe it was Jamie who pulled in closer to Liv.

One of the spelunkers called out. "Water!"

Rob took a few paces closer to the hole, bent forward, and said, "Got anything?"

"You mean, a floater?" One of them called back.

"Language," Rob said, for Jamie's benefit. "We got family here, idiot."

"Sorry, boss. Nah. Don't see anything. Not that I could. Too murky. Lots of detritus, stinks like hell. Water width about four feet and narrowing but no, uh, what should I say? Body?"

Jamie shifted and turned away.

"Liv," she said, but didn't continue.

"Shh," she said. Then Liv sighed and didn't respond.

"Ascend!" Rob called.

"Check!" One of the two spelunkers called back.

Jamie and Liv shifted when Rob came toward them. Their bodies separating made it feel to Jamie like she was tearing away from a conjoined twin.

Was I breathing?

Rob said, "If he was down there, they'd a found him."

Jamie spoke first. "Oh, okay. But Rob, if, you know, he was down there, wouldn't he sink?"

"Not without help." He squinted to explain. "Like a weight.

Anyways," he said, "bodies usually float unless they drown and then they end up coming up again too from bloating. If he broke his neck, for instance, on the way down, he'd be floating."

Liv and Jamie turned to one another. Liv's freckles had disappeared again.

"So, what's all this mean?" she said.

And again, he smirked. "What exactly is your interest here, Liv?"

A sharp, "Rob," from Jamie.

He scratched his fingers from the crown of his head around his neck, grabbing at a stiff muscle there and rubbing. "Look," he said, "we'll keep searching the island. Maybe he fell into a gully somewhere and couldn't get out. Happens," he said, as if things like this were common occurrences on the island, which Jamie knew was not true. Everyone listening knew it wasn't true.

Even so, Amen.

But everyone nodded at his lie.

CHAPTER 22
NOW—September 23, 2020

It was after five in the evening when Liv drove up, her car spinning way too fast into the circular driveway. The car lurched to a stop. She left the motor idle. I could see her head turn in our direction. Rob was standing with me on the porch.

She released pressure off the brake pedal and brought the car slowly in front of the porch steps. Then, she cracked the window and called out that she'd come back later.

I couldn't help but catch the interplay between her and Rob; their eyes connected in a spark of fury until she rolled up the window again.

I lifted my hands, questioning without calling to her why she felt she needed to leave but she hotfooted it out of the driveway with her engine throttling east, back the way she came, closer to town, north on Cattle Point Road.

A steady, gentle breeze was blowing in autumn. The afternoon fanned a crispness into the air—a cool hand swiping over the nape of my hot neck. Trees and shrubs all wore requisite seasonal colors; brushstrokes of gold, orange, cherry red painting the landscape, contrasting with deep greens in the fir trees and cedars—the blush of fall on the cheeks of the season, and a scent unmistakable to fall, a barbecue burning at one of the neighbor's homes. It was football season after all. Larry used to say that football was never any good without a good rack of ribs slathered in red sauce.

Rob stepped nearer. I wrapped one arm around my stomach and stepped back. I placed my free hand under my chin, hoping I hadn't insulted him by moving away.

"You two are very close," he said.

I nodded and gave a weak grin.

"Can I ask you something personal?" he said.

And what in the hell am I supposed to say to that? No, Mr. Deputy. You can't ask me any further questions. Or better: You're not done prying yet? No, I refuse to answer any more of your questions?

"Sure," I said.

"Is it, um. How do I say it? An *intimate* friendship?"

I hadn't expected the question. "What?" I couldn't help feeling anger in every wrinkle of the frown.

"Sorry," he said.

"No. I mean. Why would you think that?"

"Well, like I said. You two seem *really* close." His eyes accentuated the word *really*.

"I'm, well, I married, Rob. How can you think something like that?"

"And the thing with Afon."

"What *thing* with Afon?" My words were loud. Angry.

"I thought," he said. But I cut him off.

"Well, you thought *wrong*. Rob."

"I thought I saw you two one day..." he didn't finish his thought.

How could you have seen us?

"Seen us?" I asked, repeating his words. "Where would you have *seen* us? We only see each other at the library." I knew I sounded defensive and angry, but I didn't care. "What the hell are you getting at, Rob?"

They always suspect the spouse.

"Look. Sorry to upset. But you were running together, and I thought I saw you two..."

"You thought wrong!" I turned in a half circle. When I turned back to him, his face had gone white and feeble. His eyes searching and worried. "What?" A sharp demand.

He stumbled over his words. "Um, nothing. It's nothing." After he spoke, he cleared his throat. The tan in his skin returned suddenly. His eyes danced, which infuriated me.

What the hell game was he playing?

"I have to go." I set my hand on the doorknob then said, "You do too." It wasn't a suggestion but an edict.

Inside the door, his presence looming, exhaustion pooled into my feet. With my back against the doorframe, his keys and other gear clattered as he clomped down the stairs.

I didn't move off the door until I heard his car door shut, his engine turn over, and him leave my property.

CHAPTER 23
NOW—September 23, 2020

I nearly tripped over Lester who had taken up real estate on the carpeted runner lying between the hallway and the kitchen. I was racing to my cell phone.

After four chimes, Afon's phone went to voice mail. I hung up. I paced around excoriating Rob, excoriating Afon, excoriating myself.

After calming down, pouring a glass of wine to settle my nerves, and watching the clock—thirty minutes gone—I called him back.

On the second chime, someone, not Afon, spoke in a low voice and said, "Hello, James." Just like Afon would but it wasn't Afon.

"Who is this? Where's Afon?"

"Come on, Jamie. You don't recognize my voice by now?"

My scalp turned to ice; my heart thunked like a mallet striking a gong.

It was *Rob*.

"Rob."

"There ya go," he said. Pride greasing the skin around each of his words.

"Where's Afon?" I asked.

"Jamie, I thought you said you two didn't have a thing."

"We don't."

"Then why the call? To calibrate your stories?"

Calibrate? Who says stuff like that?

"There is no *story*, Rob. Now, let me speak with Afon?"

"Afon isn't here. EMS just whisked him away."

"What happened?"

"Not sure. Looks suspicious though."

"How so?"

"It's an open investigation. Can't discuss it with anyone outside law enforcement. Can't risk a dismissal in court by telling someone, even you James, about it right now. Jamie, if anyone should know that, you should." He struck an official air.

He was pissing me off royally. "Rob," I said. "Is he okay?"

"Doesn't look good. Lost a lot of blood."

"Where is he?"

"Here at the ER. They may air-evac him to St. Joe's."

Did he just chuckle?

"Ohmygod."

"Yeah. Like I said, it's pretty bad. I was just checking his phone when you called. He has some pics of you two."

I ignored him. He was trying to reel me into something.

"Can I go see him?"

"Not sure. You'd have to go to the ER and ask them."

"I'm leaving right now."

"I can meet you there?"

"No." It came out too fast. I turned down the frantic, and said, "I'd rather go alone."

"Just a thought."

"Look, Rob. I gotta go. Later." And I hung up while he was saying goodbye.

Within seconds, he called back. "Now, that wasn't nice. Hanging up on me while I was trying to be nice."

"Rob, I have no idea what's going on with you but I'm walking to my car right now. And if you didn't remember, talking on the phone and driving is against the law in Washington State. Goodbye."

I dug in my purse and located the garage door opener but fumbled it between my fingers and dropped it. The plastic case broke open and the lithium battery hung out on the concrete like a tooth that needed pulling.

After putting the opener back together, I pressed it, but the door failed to open.

Dammit.

I used the opener at the side door instead. The tambour door cranked and groaned open. A rush of air entered the garage's cavern and brought a cloud of dust off the floor into my face.

While wiping grit out of my eyes, I hurried into the car and nearly scraped the exterior paint trying to get out.

I decided to sit and take in five deep breaths. After collecting myself, I drove to the hospital.

CHAPTER 24
NOW—September 23, 2020

"Are you family?"

A thirty-something man wearing a green face mask and scrubs sat at the nurse's station checking Afon's chart. He raised his eyes to mine when I didn't answer. He looked tired, his brown eyes humorless and dull with attitude.

Why had I come at all? It wasn't like I even liked Afon all that much. Maybe it was part disbelief and part compassion for another human. Who knows? And yet, there I was, trying to get in his room to see him.

"Well?" he pressed.

The sun plastered a monolithic orange swatch on a wall behind him spanning three stories tall. The clock on that same wall showed the hour was closing in on six p.m.

"No. We're just, um, good friends."

My words muffled under my face mask. But he must have seen in my eyes the lie.

"Says here no one but family. COVID and all."

"But I'm as good as family," I said.

What the hell was I doing? Why was I lying to this person? Why did I need to be there at all?

"Sorry, ma'am. I'm not authorized to let you see him."

As I was about to state my case further, I heard a set of footsteps come up behind me.

"It's okay," a man said behind me. His voice also muffled by a face mask. Still, I knew it was Rob before I swung around to face him.

"You know he has no family here. What the hell, Rob?"

"She's with me," he told the male nurse.

He grabbed my arm to lead me to Afon. I jerked from his grip.

"Don't touch me."

"Now. Now," he said. He gave a sheepish grin to the nurse.

The nurse didn't seem to care one way or the other and went back to his work, ignoring us completely.

When I saw Afon's room was Room 7, my mood brightened. Seven was the lucky number. But when we entered, he was unresponsive and unconscious. He looked dead.

Doctors had wrapped his head in gauze. He'd been strung up with tubes and wires leading from his body to bags of fluid and blood, to a urinary drain bag, to a blood pressure monitor that led to a cuff around his upper right arm, to an EKG machine with five double leads to different areas of his body—his upper chest, upper arms, stomach, upper thighs, and ankles. And finally, they had intubated Afon with an oxygen machine which animated airflow, inhaling and exhaling, as it forced air into his lungs.

"Oh my God," I kept my voice low. "Is he going to make it?"

"They're giving him a fifty-fifty chance," Rob said.

A young female nursing assistant walked in. She was Hispanic and thin. We stepped away from Afon's bed to let her in. She replaced a drain bag with an empty one and left the room.

"What happened to him?"

"Head injury."

"How?"

"Under investigation. I told you. I can't say."

I walked over to the side of his bed and grabbed Afon's arm. His skin felt cool. "He needs more covers."

"They know what they're doing, Jamie."

"Are they going to take him to Bellingham?"

"If he stabilizes, they will move him. Until then, they're going to keep him here." Rob paused for a moment then added, "It was lucky they had the brain guy here this week."

"Brain guy?"

"Head injury doc. His specialty."

"Aw," I said.

"It was all over the newspaper. I'm surprised you missed it. It's pretty big news for our little island."

"I guess I've had other things on my mind," I said.

He couldn't ignore the attitude in my statement. He knew what I meant, about having to identify Larry by only his foot and shoe.

"'Course. How insensitive of me. Sorry, James."

"Don't call me that. That was Afon's thing." I squeezed Afon's arm. "He and Liv are the only ones who can call me that now. If you don't mind."

"Are you in love with him?"

The question stumped me. I stumbled over my thoughts. "Of course not," I said.

And I didn't love him. It was a ridiculous question. Still, we had history but nothing romantic. Not ever.

"I don't believe you." He said it in a sing-songy way like a child.

"Oh please. Give me a break. How old are you anyway, and by the way, what's it matter to you if I liked Afon or not? I did like Afon. He was a pain in the ass sometimes, but he was a friend. I liked him fine but not the way you're thinking. How sick."

I walked out, leaving Rob behind. Why had I been referring to Afon as someone I knew from the past.

A few seconds later I heard Rob's shoes scrape the floor outside of Afon's room. He called out to me, but I wasn't about to stop. Wouldn't stop. Not for Rob.

That is, not until the hospital's alarm system went off and someone over the sound system called for a "code blue."

"Code Blue," a female nurse called over the intercom system. "Room 7."

CHAPTER 25
NOW—September 23, 2020

"Jesus Christ!"

"Liv, *please* don't say that in front of me," I said.

"Sorry, but Jamie, this is surreal."

We were on a Zoom chat. Her face in two-dimension flatness on my laptop monitor. Her skin and hair fuzzed among the pixels and when she spoke, her voice followed her words, squealing out at times, not matching with her lips, her facial expression, or her head movement.

I'd fixed a bowl of ramen noodles that I'd ordered for the lockdown in March, six months before. I still had another case in the garage. I was eating while we talked.

"It's bad," I said between each spoonful of soup.

"Is he going to make it?"

Liv's eyes darkened when I shook my head. Then, I said, "I don't know."

Liv took in a breath again.

But she had more questions about Afon:

> Did Rob tell me what happened? No.
> You said he had been intubated? Yes.
> Can I go see him? Not unless Rob goes with you.

To that she said, "Bleh. I'd rather have a root canal."

I chuckled. "Well, he definitely creeps me out too, but why do you hate him so much?"

She swiped a hand across her brow. "It's like he always shows up at the strangest times. Like he's threatening me somehow. Like he's watching. He watches you all the time. Haven't you noticed?"

I didn't answer the question. Instead, I said, "Maybe it's because you included him—and not so subtly I might add—in your last thriller."

She giggled. "Maybe *that's* it."

"You made him out to be the villain."

"He's the perfect embodiment for a villain, don't you think? I mean, those piercing green eyes. That square jaw. His backwoods island speak."

"I don't know," I said. "I don't think he's, how do I say it, *sophisticated* enough to be a villain."

Liv chuckled. "Those ones are the worst," she said. "They come off unsophisticated but then, boom, they've been planning a crime all along."

"You're writing something right this second in your head, aren't you?"

She laughed. "I am!" Her face darkened again. "Maybe you could go with me?"

"They wouldn't let me in without Rob. And one more thing about Rob, he *was* pretty embarrassed by all the talk around here. You know what Steph said."

"About getting a lawyer to sue me? Pish-posh. Nothing to sue. Anyway, too bad about his feelings. Besides, the copyright disclaimer explicitly states that all persons, places, and events are fictional."

If I wasn't looking into her eyes, I'd have sworn she was reading the disclaimer in the book.

Then she added, "Anyway, it's not like he cares much about other people's feelings."

"You talking about the guy in jail?"

Liv nodded.

"That's folklore. Never happened," I said.

"Don't be so sure."

Right then, Paul passed behind her, backed up, and stuck his face down into view. "Hey Jamie, how've you been these days?"

"Hey Paul. You know. Getting by."

"Well, you know, we're here for you." He pulled Liv in tight.

"I do, and I appreciate it, Paul. Thank you."

"Okay," he said, and blew me a kiss.

"You are both so lucky to have each other," I said to Liv.

She nodded. "The luckiest."

Paul got her attention from off the screen. She nodded to him and held up a finger. Then, she said, "He needs me in the garden. Will you keep me posted on Afon?"

"I will, Mary, Mary, quite contrary."

Liv giggled and said goodbye. Then our Zoom chat screen went blank.

For some wicked time after our chat, I kept humming *Mary, Mary, quite contrary*. It became an earworm that I couldn't shake from my thoughts. It niggled me the entire rest of the day until later when I got more bad news in a text.

CHAPTER 26
NOW—September 23, 2020

Freaking *Mary, Mary*, the nursery rhyme replayed and replayed in my mind until ten minutes to one in the morning when I finally refused to lie down in bed. I sat against every pillow on the bed, Larry's too. Lester jumped up between my calves. I had to crook them open for him to fit.

My brain scrambled from tossing Larry's clothes to cleaning the cat box. But here's the thing: I wasn't going to do what everyone told me. I wasn't about to get rid of things Larry used. I wanted reminders of him. They didn't haunt me like people thought they might. They comforted me. I wanted to keep his things close. I wanted to smell his sweaters and the hair in his brush.

I knew there'd be a time when I would relinquish his things but now wasn't the time.

I pulled the laptop over and flipped it open. The first thing that popped into view was a CGI from our satellite phone app telling me that I had a text message.

When I tapped on the CGI, the app window opened and there at the top in a list of other text messages was one from Rob. It read: "Call me."

But I didn't call. I texted him on my Facetime app: "What's going on?"

Then Rob: "Not this way. Call."

141

Me: "Number?"

After texting me his number, he wrote, "I can't believe you don't know my number by now."

It was a good thing we weren't video chatting. I didn't want him to see how much he irked me.

I dialed through the computer app. When he picked up, the first thing he said was, "You don't know my number yet?"

"Rob, what's so important that you sent me a late-night text?"

"It's Afon. He didn't make it."

Boom. There it was. I swallowed hard.

Pretty maids all in a row. First Larry. Now Afon. Who was next in line?

"Hear me?" he said.

His words jolted me back to the present. "Yes. I heard. I need to go."

"Where?" he said.

"No, not *where*, I just need to get off the call."

"You can cry if you want to. I won't mind. But if you ask me, he doesn't deserve your sympathy."

Ohmygod. What was wrong with him?

"Rob, I gotta go. Okay?" I didn't want to hang up on him again. "I'll call you later in the morning."

He breathed heavy through the receiver. "I guess." He paused, but said, "Sure you'll remember my number?" Then he hung up.

My hands began to shake. Afon was dead. I could barely type.

I shot a note to Liv telling her to contact me as soon as she could and was surprised that she saw the message within seconds of me entering it.

"'S'up buttercup?"

"It's Afon."

"Oh no. What?"

"He didn't make it," I wrote.

She didn't respond immediately. I imagined her getting out of bed so as not to disturb Paul, walking to their living room, pouring a shot of whiskey and pausing before typing her response. It took that long anyway.

"Were you awake?" I typed.

"Couldn't sleep."

"Something about this night. Me too. Couldn't sleep."

"His spirit. Telling us both he was leaving."

"Oh my God, Liv. Stop."

She paused.

"It's true," she texted back. "Why on earth were we both awake?"

"A song in my brain."

Another pause. This one longer. Then finally...

"Mary, Mary, quite contrary?" she asked.

My skin went cold.

Finally, I typed: "OMG. Yes."

Liv: "Told you. His spirit."

"Liv, I'll call you later today."

"Did Rob tell you?"

"Yes."

"I'm telling you. Afon's spirit is trying to tell us something."

"I don't know why I'm so upset."

"He was a total ass, but he was still a human being."

I paused for a second before I wrote. "Was that it? Was that all? He was human? Didn't we care about him for more than that?"

"You still there?" she wrote.

"Yeah. Sorry. Look, I'll call later," I wrote.

"Later," she responded.

Then, I shut my laptop and sat in the dark two more hours, until dawn snuck up on the black night—when the gray of morning split a line across the horizon.

CHAPTER 27
THEN—June 21, 2020

"Like I said, we'll keep searching the island."

Liv had jumped into her car and was heading out the drive by the time Rob and Jamie reached the porch. It seemed lately they were always ending up standing in front of her door together.

As if he picked up on this very thought, he said, "I end up here with you a lot, don't I? On the porch." But then he went on, "It's a homey place. Comfortable. I can see why you love it here."

Without thinking, she said, "Larry and I used to sit out here all the time." A smile ending her words.

But he jumped on her smile. "Yeah, well, that was then, wasn't it?"

Jamie couldn't believe the insensitivity of his words. "Excuse me?" she said.

He rubbed a hand over his buzz cut. "Look, I'll get back with you. If we hear or see anything."

He seemed to walk slower than he had before, like a kid who got caught peeking through some girl's bedroom window.

He was walking away, talking to the woods not to her, when he said, "You look tired, Jamie Michaels. You could use a good night's sleep."

After turning into the house, Jamie hoped Rob paused after hearing the door close behind her.

PRETTY MAIDS
ALL IN A ROW—Now

CHAPTER 28
NOW—September 24, 2020

It was five thirty when I read the article the next morning. After feeding Lester and getting another cup of tea, I had scanned the online newspaper to see if they had posted anything yet.

Sure enough, they had.

I texted Liv again that the article about Afon's death had gone live and was online.

It read:

Well-known retired orthopedic surgeon Afon Daniels was found in his home Tuesday, September 22, with extensive head injuries. The injuries did not appear accidental. Authorities say that the information they gathered to this point suggests someone entered his home before 5:30 p.m., September 23. A struggle ensued. Dr. Daniels was found severely beaten. He remained on life support at PeaceHealth Peace Island Medical Center in Friday Harbor until his condition worsened in the early hours of September 24. He was transported via helicopter to St. Joseph's Hospital in Bellingham, Washington where he was pronounced dead at 1:33 a.m. He is survived by ex-wife Sandra (Daniels) McMurtry, who lives in Austin, Texas.

Daniels' body will be transported back to the San Juan County coroner for an autopsy and determination of cause of death. The body will be cremated at Raven's Mortuary in Anacortes, Washington.

McMurtry stated they would not be holding a local service in Friday Harbor and instead would be planning services in Houston. In lieu of flowers, Mrs. Daniels has asked for donations to go to the Austin Women's Shelter.

Mrs. McMurtry seemed to be getting a final dig in at her late ex-husband. I wondered how many times he'd fooled around on her. How many times he'd pushed the envelope on his advances with other women.

I wondered about Steph, whether she knew.

I wondered about her relationship with Afon and her own husband, Tom.

Then I stopped wondering and decided to give her a call.

CHAPTER 29
NOW—September 24, 2020

"Jamie, what time is it?" Steph's voice was raspy from sleep.

The thing about women friends: we stay thick as thieves even when we've had trouble in the past; even when we want to hurt the other one, women friends have the capacity to forgive. We may never forget but we'll forgive and remain tight. It's like a biological loyalty. But with every loyalty there are limits.

This morning, all Steph and my trouble faded to the background. She needed to hear the news from one of her female friends.

It's different with women and men friends. Women will turn on a man and kick him to the curb as fast as you can say menopause.

Liv and I had stopped texting before dawn. I'd been up for hours and hadn't thought that people might still be sleeping. I checked the time. It was only 5:38.

"Oh God, Steph. I'm sorry. I lost track of the time. I've been up since around one this morning."

"What in God's name for?"

"Did I wake Tom?"

"What do you think?" she said. After a moment, she regrouped, then said, "Sorry about the 'tude," No doubt using one of her teenaged daughter's phrases. "He's in the bathroom. He's exhausted. His car broke down and he got all banged up trying to fix it. He's in a mood. Anyway, what's up?"

"So, you haven't heard?"

"Oh God, Jamie. The drama," she said. "Look, I've been *asleep*. I haven't *heard* anything."

I waited enough time that she asked if I was still there.

"Yeah, right. I'm sorry. Look, I'm sorry about calling so early, Steph, but it's online now, the news. The local news." I didn't want to come right out and say: *Afon's dead.*

Instead, I eased into it by saying, "It's about Afon."

"Oh God, now what? What'd he do?"

"Steph, he didn't *do* anything." I thought about how they did it on *Law & Order*, how they'd first say, *there's been an accident,* but there had been no accident.

"There was a break-in," I said instead.

"Where?" she asked.

"Afon's."

A silent understanding fell between us.

"Are you there?" I asked.

"Is he..."

"Oh, Steph. I'm so sorry. He was badly injured. He didn't make it, Steph."

I heard her throat catch. A silent pause filled the call. I imagined tears draining from Steph's eyes absent any weeping.

In the background, I heard Tom ask, "What's wrong?" It sounded like he was some stranger just passing through, like he really didn't care.

She didn't answer him. She sniffled. There was a slight moan behind it. She was crying.

Now, Tom asked again, sounding more gruff than compassionate.

Then the phone went dead.

"Shit," I said. Lester cocked back his ears. He stayed tuned into my sounds. Kept a keen eye on my emotions. I stopped mid-stroke on his back when Lester turned to me. He looked like a cat who wanted to say something. It was in the glow of his eyes. He didn't need to do anything else; not rant, not scream. His golden eyes said everything.

They told me, If anyone has a reason to kill Afon, it's Tom!

SARCOPHAGUS—Then & Now

CHAPTER 30
NOW—September 25, 2020

Steph's words distorted in the phone. She was frantic. I could barely make out what she was saying.

First, "Tom!" Afterward a muddle of words strung together, discombobulated.

"Steph, your mouth is too close."

Inconsolable tears.

I let her cry and kept my peace. Between sobs, she got out what she had been trying to tell me all along: Rob came with two deputies and took Tom in.

"They handcuffed him!"

They were charging him with Afon's murder. It was Friday evening so Tom's arraignment wouldn't be until Monday at nine o'clock in the morning. He'd have to spend the weekend incarcerated.

"I'll be right over," I said.

Steph refused. She had to call their lawyer and meet Tom down at the station.

"What can I do?" I said.

"There's nothing to do."

Lester bounced up onto the counter and headbutted me. I looked at him with a growl in my eyes.

Before she ended our call, Steph laughed but without humor. It was the laugh of someone who believed the world had turned against her. It was a stunned sound.

There were two doors for Steph, one with prizes and money and fame: the one she'd been living in today. Then, there was the other door with a bag of dog dung in a flaming sack on her porch. She'd somehow stepped out that door and into the dung, and now she couldn't understand how life had turned against her.

A fragment of something we don't like to admit, something unkind, poked its face into my consciousness. The face wore a comedy-tragedy mask. I wanted to shoo it away. But it muscled in.

Right then, I realized that there were two doors for me now also. One etched with a wooden sign reading: *Pity for Steph*. Yet another with a sign that read: *Vindicated*.

Where had my female loyalty gone? Was it when Steph took advantage of Larry? If so, that would be a good reason. But maybe it was something else. Maybe I had wanted a fast little fling with Afon and wasn't admitting it to myself until now.

That seemed ridiculous. I loved Larry. I missed him so much I felt it in my bones.

So, I refused to open either door. Not at least while I was still on the phone with Steph.

But when we hung up, I knew which door I would walk through.

CHAPTER 31
NOW—September 25, 2020

Liv and I sat on one of the court's pews immediately behind Steph, who was seated between a team of lawyers. It was the arraignment hearing.

"We're doing the right thing, that's why," Liv said.

"She doesn't deserve anyone's pity," I said.

Liv hushed me when the prosecutor asked for remand. He argued that Tom had already spent three days incarcerated and couldn't see why he shouldn't remain there. He had the wherewithal to abscond from the island and get to another country, he insinuated, one possibly without an extradition treaty with the US.

Tom's defense attorney argued against remand stating that his businesses were here and that he had been a beacon in the community. His roots were here on the island and to leave would mean to leave his loving wife (I squeezed Liv's hand at that), his business, and his entire life.

The judge went for the prosecutor's request. Judges tend to favor prosecutors.

There was a flurry of discussion between Tom and his defense attorney until the attorney patted his shoulder, nodded, and allowed the bailiff to take him back to his cell.

Steph's head drooped to her chest. Liv touched her shoulder, rubbed it.

She said, "Steph, whatever you need. We're here for you."

Everyone says that to people in times of trouble. But when you look around for help, who's really there? But when Liv said it, it rang true to me.

Steph arose when the attorney approached.

We sat back when they began to speak, their voices discreet and conspiratorial.

The judge called to the bailiff, "Next?"

Liv pulled out a small notebook, a journal, and started taking down notes. She was gathering observations for a future scene, perhaps. I nudged her. Didn't want Steph to see.

"What?" she said. The word took on a tone of defense.

Part of me wanted to stop her. And when I saw her masks appear—one comedy, the other tragedy—I let the issue drop.

When my attention returned to the back of Steph's head, I noticed a patch of her highlighted hair tangled as if she had just gotten out of bed. If I'd had a comb handy, I might have dragged it across the tangle.

I was laser-focused on her hair when Rob slid in next to me.

He whispered across to Liv, "Enjoying the show?"

She refused to comment and lifted her middle finger at him.

I said, "How could you, Rob?"

"How could I what?"

"Tom would never do something like this."

The judge and a whole new set of attorneys stepped up. A young man with tattoos covering both his arms. The judge's voice and attorneys' droned in the background.

"How can you know what people are capable of? How can anyone ever know?" he said.

He kept his face stern and close, only inches from mine. The irises in his eyes dilated. "Hmm?" he said.

I pulled away and inched closer to Liv, who scooted, allowing some space between us. Rob sat back.

"Why do you two care so much? About Tom *or* Afon?"

"They're our friends, Rob." I shook my head in disbelief that he could even pose the question. "What's wrong with you?"

Liv chuckled under her breath but kept writing, trying to ignore us.

"With me? Oh man, that's rich." He laughed. "Nothing's wrong with me, Jamie. You'll find that out in short order but don't make me out to be the bad guy."

"Tom's not a killer," I said.

"Takes one to know one," he said.

Liv stopped writing. She leaned against the pew but kept her face forward.

"What does *that* mean?"

My voice pitched up. The judge turned in our direction, taking note.

"Sorry, Your Honor," Rob said. "It's nothing."

The judge scowled and looked down to his docket.

Rob turned his focus back to me. "You two need to leave."

Liv said, "We don't have to leave if we don't want to. It's a public proceeding."

We swapped a brief, loveless exchange, then Liv continued scribbling down notes.

Rob grabbed my hand. I pulled my hand free. Liv nudged me. She leaned in and whispered, "He wants you bad."

I shifted left, closer to Liv. Rob turned to us. He placed one hand on the back of the pew with Steph and one on ours.

"Look, Tom's lawyer has this. You can't help her right now."

"We're here for support."

Rob rubbed a hand over his hair and stood. Then, he stepped out of the court's pew but stopped short of walking off.

He bent forward and whispered, "Want to go get some coffee with me?"

Liv's head cocked but she didn't stop writing. She whispered loud enough for him to hear, "Told ya."

I whispered back, "No. Rob. I'm staying here. For Steph. Remember? Support?"

"Okay. Sure. Whatever," he said. And made like he was going to walk off but stopped and returned. He bent his face to mine.

"Can I ask you something personal, Jamie?"

"What now?"

"Were you in love with Afon?"

I felt all the blood from my feet and legs surge into my face. But I couldn't confirm or deny the question. Steph turned slightly away from Tom, who was still standing in front of the judge.

"Oh my God," I said.

Rob straightened his back and looked down on me. He squinted.

"That's not a refusal," he said. He squinted at me harder.

I flustered and said, "Of course not."

After he took off, Liv leaned in and put her mouth so close to my ear I could feel the skin on her lips.

"He's so into you that his pants are tight."

"Shut up," I said, pulling away from her.

She raised her eyebrows and nodded. "Maybe that's good," she said. Still, keeping her voice low. "Maybe it will prove to be useful."

And maybe she was right. Maybe it would prove a useful tool for the future.

But then again, maybe it was the worst thing that could ever happen.

CHAPTER 32
NOW—September 25, 2020

Rest in peace, Larry.

On Rob's suggestion and "because of safety issues," he'd said, I hired a contractor to shore up the sides of the crevice and build a metal structure over the crack that spanned six feet wide in all directions. The contractors were grinding away at the earth, chewing holes deep in the rock's core to anchor the structure. When they finished, the metal would fit like the armor of an armadillo over the hole. Moveable. Flexing when the earth moved. Stretching, shrinking, heaving, whatever the earth wished.

The sound of my work boots crushing pine cones, twigs, gravel over the trail to the crevice added a sultry tempo to our walk back toward the house and Rob's cop car.

We were heading away from the crevice, Rob and I. Eyes down tracking our steps over the woodland ground. It was a solemn moment. We weren't speaking until all of a sudden we were, both at the same time.

He said my name as I said his.

"You first," I said. We'd both chuckled but nothing seemed funny to me. Rob either. He was quieter today than I'd ever seen him.

"No, you," he said, deferring to let me speak first.

"Well, I was thinking. You know, after all of this. Well, all of everything. I decided I'm going to sell this place. I just can't..."

"And do what? Buy closer to town? 'Cause if you need a place to stay..." His words hung in the air like a torn spiderweb from its anchor.

I interrupted. Fearing what he was about to offer, I said, "No." It came out too fast and hard. So, I repeated more gently, "No, I'm. Uh, leaving the island."

My face flushed with blood and my cheeks went hot. I shoved my hands into my back pockets and snagged my cuticle on the contractor's business card. Refusing to meet his eyes, I noticed from my peripheral when his face darted in my direction.

"Leave, huh?" he said.

"You know, Rob. Too many bad memories."

He lifted his face. His eyes searching the tops of firs that lined the path, to the tips of alders and the crowns of cedars.

A Northern Flicker and a robin competed for airtime. The robin's lilting soft tune stabbed through and through by the flicker's coarse jabbing call. The smell of someone's fireplace hit my stomach with lingering notes of beef and mushroom intertwined.

We didn't speak until we reached the porch.

Rob said, "I don't like that you think you're gonna leave." He fumbled inside one of his front pockets. He pulled out his hand. It was fisted as if he were holding something in his palm but when we heard the rumbling of a car engine entering the driveway, he stuffed his fist back into his pocket.

CHAPTER 33
NOW—September 25, 2020

Liv popped over. When I peered through the glass in the door, I could tell she had been crying.

A tell-tale heart does not die softly.

I flew open the door. "Get in here," I said. "What's wrong?" And I followed her into the den where she crumpled onto the red chair where I typically sat and prayed. It was a holy place. Maybe some of it would rub off on Liv...on me at some point in our lives.

"I can't do it any longer," she said.

I knew what she meant. She couldn't keep the secret. Now, what? It was on her advice we did what we did. I believed her. Believed they would charge me with murder. It wasn't my first choice. I wanted to call the authorities, but Liv talked me out of doing so. And now, she wants to renege?

"I see," was all I could say.

"I'm going to the sheriff tomorrow, Jamie. I'm so sorry but I just can't hold it in any longer. I intend to tell them that it was me who talked you into this whole mess."

That was where the truth had begun, and this lie is where it would all end.

On one hand, a certain relief washed over me. On the other, it didn't sound nearly as innocent as it had been when we joined forces in this charade—a charade I wasn't sure I wanted to end.

If and when they found Larry's body...

But they aren't going to find his body. Not unless they hire amphibious spelunkers and they would have to believe they knew where his body was to do that.

...So far, Rob hadn't told her about any amphibious spelunkers. But then again, Rob wasn't saying much these days.

I had to stop her. But before I tried to dissuade her from the idea, someone knocked at the door.

My eyes mirrored Liv's. Fear and panic all pouring out—cornucopias spilling out the fruits of truth from our eyes.

"Shit," she said. She put a hand to her mouth. Her freckles blended into a sudden blush. Her hazel eyes, watery.

Somehow, my body took over. I don't remember rising but there I was, looking down on Liv. "Wait here." The order came out harsher than I had intended. So, I said, "I'll try to get rid of whoever's at the door."

CHAPTER 34
NOW—June 20, 2020

Seeing Larry teetering at the top of the stairs felt like some morbid magic trick. He was there one second and gone the next. She almost tumbled down herself racing down to get to him.

Was she already crying? Screaming his name? Her wild breathing was choppy, erratic. His head hung oddly. The angle all off. Crooked and out of place. A broken neck.

The groaning house still groaned but now at a higher pitch. How big was this earthquake? Until the reverberation settled closer to Larry, and it was only then she realized the high timbre was coming from her gut, from her throat. She was screaming his name. Once, twice, more. More than she could count. The words warbled and buckled under her tears. What had she done? What had she done?

But she had done nothing. She hadn't caused the fall. But when he reached for her, she shrank away. Didn't help. Hid her hands behind her back.

She had spent the last two years constantly helping Larry—cleaning up after incontinence—both fecal and urinary—helping him into and out of chairs, changing the sheets when he wet the bed, helped him into the shower, showered him, dried him off, clothed him, helped him up and down the stairs, made three meals a day for him, fed him, made him drink three bottles of water daily, gave him his medications morning, noon, and night, helped him blow his nose, took him to the doctor, to the store, walked him to the bathroom, and helped him into bed.

Not because she had to because she wanted to. She loved Larry. But she wanted him to recover. For his mind to suddenly heal. For God to wave his magic wand over Larry's skull and say, "You are healed." She loved him as much that day as she did when they got married, when his mind was right and he could speak without pointing to things he'd forgotten the names of. For him to wake up one morning and have reverted back to good old Larry. For them to live out their lives together as if the few years of dementia had been some medical hoax. Some anomaly. She'd even ordered an emergency identification device if he stole away and got lost, which she slipped off his neck at the bottom of the stairs. Which she hung on the bathroom door where he showered so that it would appear as though he took the thing off and simply forgot to put it back on, then left the house without it. But there he was. Her precious Larry. Her angry, funny, forgetful Larry.

She checked his neck and cried when she felt no pulse. She laid one hand on his chest. So still. Put her ear to his heart. Silent.

When she awoke, it was because someone was at the door. Knocking. Calling her name. How long had she been lying there? It wasn't dark. But the knocking.

She pushed up off Larry's body.

"Oh my God!"

It was Liv. She was looking down at them both lying there at the bottom of the stairs. She hadn't noticed them on the floor before until Jamie raised up.

Liv pushed through the door and in doing so, shoved Larry inches away from it. And it must have hit her, the smell—a mix of feces and urine—the letting go of all fluids held inside of Larry's body had released, when she said, "Ohmygod." And covered her mouth.

"Jamie! What happened?"

She wiped her face and answered, "The earthquake. He was at the top of the stairs."

"Is he?" Liv didn't need to say the word *dead*. Jamie understood and began crying again. Liv helped her off Larry and walked her to the den to sit. She grabbed a glass of water.

"Drink this."

Jamie obeyed like a child.

"Liv," she said, "they'll think I did it."

"No, they won't."

Jamie rolled her eyes. And then nodded without speaking.

Liv sat next to her and shifted her body to face front, to think, Jamie suspected. To view something neutral—anything—the red leather chair, the bronze floor lamp, the books on the shelves. There were so many mysteries and thrillers. So many where a loved one was implicated in the killing of a spouse.

"Shit," Liv said. It seemed she came to the same conclusion as Jamie. What else could she do? She wrote those stories. Research alone proved that the spouse was always implicated in the murder of another spouse and charged and convicted more often than not.

"No one needs to know."

"What?" Jamie couldn't believe what Liv was saying. "I have to tell his family. He has children, brothers, friends. What? Is he just going to up and disappear? Poof! Vanish!? Come on. I have to call the sheriff's department or 9-1-1. Both."

And it was in that second, the beat of a butterfly wing against Liv's lashes, that Jamie understood.

"Liv. We can't."

Her face took on a look of resolve. "He *can* go missing."

Liv set out the plan. The island was all abuzz, she'd said, about the earthquake. That's why she showed up. She had worried about Jamie and Larry. Was worried about their gas appliances. Paul, her own husband, hurried her out of the house when he saw she was concerned about Jamie. Paul and she made quick work at their own home, turning everything off. He said he didn't need her and to go. Then there were some explosions. EMS was dispatched. No one would know the wiser. Liv had said. It would fall into the flotsam of others who got injured or died because of the earthquake.

"We'll go as planned to the book club. People will be excited and nervous. You'll fit right in."

She spoke as she tapped something into her cell. "I'm texting everyone and telling them nothing's changed. That we're still going to the library. The only thing different, and really not so much, will be that I drove you. Okay?"

Jamie couldn't believe she was going to agree. "So, we just leave him here?"

"No! No matter what, it has to look like he walked off and got lost."

"Why can't we just leave him here and I can call when we get home. Say I found him."

"Body temp. Lividity. Will all point to him dying well before the meeting. You have no alibi for before, but you would for during."

"Ohmygod, Liv." Jamie began to cry again and reached for Larry. His body was cold. "When was the earthquake?"

She checked her cell and read. "Three-thirty-seven. 6.7 magnitude." She began to read the coordinates then bagged the idea. "Right. Directly. Under the island."

Then it occurred to her. Liv was right, the authorities would think she pushed him.

They always suspect the spouse. Always.

Together they scanned each step. No sign of blood. No skin. A scuff mark here and there but nothing that appeared out of place. Except of course for Larry's body at the bottom of the stairs. Definitely not normal.

His urine and bowel contents would be easy to clean. Blood wasn't easy to get rid of. Things Liv told her. Things she knew before Liv told her.

And after they charted out a few more details, they went on to deal with Larry's body.

CHAPTER 35
NOW—September 25, 2020

Liv stood when Rob walked in with me. He was carrying a bottle inside a brown paper bag.

"I'll cut to the chase," he said. But thinking again, he said, "Wait. First, I think this deserves a toast, Jamie. Let's drink a toast."

"I'm driving," Liv said.

"Oh pish-posh," he said. "Get us some wine," he said to me.

I stood my ground. He shrugged and said, "Glad I brought this then." And he held up the bag and slipped out a bottle of Dom Perignon. "Glasses, at least?" he said.

Liv and I remained quiet. Rob followed me to a cupboard where I kept champagne glasses.

When I pulled them out, he said, "That should do nicely."

He popped the cork. It hit the ceiling. Champagne burbled out, forming a small arc and spilling onto the floor. Rob whooped. Lester skulked out of the room. His feet padding fast up the stairs.

"I always wanted to do that," he said.

I glanced over to Liv. She was glaring.

I grabbed a towel off the gas stove, but Rob snatched it out of my hand, wiped off the neck of the bottle, then dropped it at his feet, where a pool of wine began to grow concentrically outward.

Rob poured the wine into all three champagne flutes and handed us our glasses before picking up his and raising his arm.

"To when Larry left us," he said.

I set my glass down.

Liv stood, walked to the sink, and poured out her glass.

"Oh, come on, gals. No sense of humor? This was expensive." He took a sip and grimaced. "Not all that great." He nearly began to laugh. "Look. We all know what happened to Larry. And we all have a little secret, the three of us, don't we? That kinda makes us partners, doesn't it?"

Liv's eyes burned red and she began to cry.

"See, Jamie? Now, that's a guilty conscience. I see it a lot in my line of work. When you see that much guilt, you learn how to conceal it. So, what's with you, Jamie? Where's your conscience been hiding?"

He bent to look straight into my eyes.

"I guess I lost any sense of guilt while I was grieving." The words came out insincere. Of course, I felt guilty, but not for murder, which I knew was what Rob was implying.

"It wasn't our fault," Liv said.

"No? Then who's fault was it?" He pulled out his cell and held up a series of photos for us to view. "Check this out. Here's where you wrap Larry's body in a tarp."

My eyes caught Liv's. They filled with knowledge as though she'd flipped through pages in the Book of Life trying to find her name listed but could not.

"The flash," I said.

"Guilty. I forgot to turn the flash off on the camera." He chuckled. "You nearly caught me, but I hid."

He flipped to the next image. "This is where you drag him to the crevice, and..." he flipped images again, "this is where you roll him off the ledge and into the hole. Oh, this is my fave. When he gets his foot caught in between the root and the boulder. Couldn'ta seen that coming." I had to turn away. But when he said, "And this is where Liv cut off his foot? Good lord.

What the hell, Liv. By the way." I looked again.

He unsnapped the shoulder holster of his gun and pulled it out with his free hand. "Hand over the knife." He took another sip and tipped his head to the taste. "You really should have some, Jamie. It's not that bad. It's had time to *aerate*. Is that the term? Aerate?" He set down his glass and held out his hand.

Liv sniffed and wiped at her nose. She unlocked her ankle holster and handed the knife to Rob, handle first. He pocketed the weapon in the back of his belt.

"This implicates you as much as it does us," I said.

"No, sweety. No, it doesn't."

"If I went to the sheriff..."

Liv jumped in. "He would simply say that this was evidence in an ongoing investigation. That he wanted to have everything wrapped up before presenting it to either the sheriff or the prosecuting attorney."

"Bingo," he said. "You are one smart authoress, Liv. Not many out there but you sure take the cake."

Then Liv asked, "Why Afon?"

He flipped his hand at her. "Collateral damage. Jamie's baggage. Couldn't have him become a problem later on down the road. Plus, he was a dick."

My hands went icy. Liv's eyes connected with mine. A death seeped into her eyes. I followed where her gaze had landed, somewhere well past the window out in the field.

The sky was dimming. A robin began calling its night call, a call that hinted of a Swainson's thrush, but the robin couldn't reach the highest note and cut off short. Still, its song sounded beautiful and juxtaposed against the conversation inside the house. A bank of clouds scudded across the sky behind our oldest tree, a Douglas fir that topped out at only forty feet when Jamie first moved there but that was now no shorter than seventy feet. From where she stood, she could only envision the uppermost branches bending in the wind with the clouds.

"Okay, enough of me being a nice guy. This is how we're going to play this."

Liv crumpled onto the couch, leaned forward with her hands smashed into her face. The subtle jerking of her shoulders was all I needed to see that she was crying.

"Paul doesn't know."

"And he never will if you both do what I say."

I opened an upper cabinet that ran along the same wall as the refrigerator and pulled out a bottle of Maker's Mark. After pulling out two tumblers, I filled both to a point just below the halfway mark. This was a *glass half empty* moment. I sat next to Liv and handed her a scotch, then proceeded to take big gulps, finally finishing it while Liv sipped at hers slowly but steadily.

"Impressive. You are intoxicating, Jamie," Rob said. Then, he said, "Get it? Intoxicating?"

I slumped back against the couch. The leather was cool but warmed up fast against my hot skin.

Behind us, Rob splashed more champagne into his glass, then sauntered to a chair, the one facing the couch, and sat. He let out a breath of self-satisfaction. Then said, "Aw," once he was seated.

The liquor warmed my chest. The lulling force of scotch tangoed between calm and frantic and loosened my tongue.

"So, how *are* we going to play this, Rob? You've obviously been planning this for a while. It must've killed you—excuse the pun—keeping it to yourself for so long. Why'd you wait all these months?"

Liv elbowed me. Her eyes pressing me to shut up.

"No, Liv. He thinks he's so smart. He thinks he knows what happened. And you know, I think he thinks this is funny."

"Not funny at all," he said. "But yes, planning for some time now. And you have to know, ladies. I intend you no harm. In fact, my plan is to do *nothing*."

I squinted at him. Not believing for a moment that all this pomp—the champagne, telling us he knew about Larry being tossed into the crevice—was devised just so he might do nothing.

"Nothing?" I said.

"That's right, Jamie. Nothing. So long as you both do nothing too. Say nothing. Not. One. Word." He glanced at Liv. "To *anyone*. Not Paul. No one. Got it? Unless you both want me to come back and deem this place a crime scene. You'd be amazed the kind of evidence we can turn up."

Liv looked at the wall next to the red gas fireplace. She kept her face pointed away from both of us.

Rob scooted forward in his seat like a common criminal in on the plan. Both hands clasping the champagne flute. "So, this is the idea…"

But Liv stood. She took a deep swig of scotch and set it on the cocktail table. "I can't." She looked at me. "Sorry, Jamie, but this is eating me up inside. I can't do this." And she turned to go but not before Rob spoke again.

"You'll keep your mouth shut or you both'll end up in prison—Jamie for murder and you as her accomplice, felony murder. Both types hold life sentences. I've thought about it long and hard," he said. "In fact, Liv, and you'll get this, it should put the proverbial period on the end of *your* sentence." He winked at me and my stomach lurched. He laughed. "First, the *photos*," he said. "You know about those."

Blood drained out of my skull and pooled somewhere down at my feet. What bravery I'd felt earlier against his suggestion to play along with his plan, left me. He had material evidence.

"But that's not all," he said. "I have my ace in the hole. So, you say a word, Miss Bestselling Author, and your best buddy here will get her sweet little ass…" He smiled at me at this point. He actually smiled. "…thrown in prison before you can say literati." With that he sat back again, crossing his left leg over his right knee and downing his champagne. It surprised me for a second, that he knew the word *literati*.

Had he been playing the Gomer role all this time? Was that

his investigative trait? To seem less intelligent to people of interest, setting them off-balance, trapping them in a lie?

"So, yes, Liv. You will keep quiet lest you both end up in the slammer and not for a year or two, no. I bet you're both happy you're living in Washington State right about now because another state, say Arizona," he paused, his eyes snapping to mine then back again, "could sentence you *both* to death." He got up to pour himself more champagne. Liv leaned against the wall, seemingly holding it up. For a moment, I worried she might fall.

But Rob didn't stop his tirade. He said, "Of course, in Arizona, when the prosecution seeks the death penalty, the sentence is decided by the jury and *must* be unanimous. But Arizona is a conservative state with a ton of Republicans down there who still believe that battle between the Earps and the cowboys in *Tombstone* was a great method of enforcing the rule of law."

"Stop," Liv said. "Please. Just stop." She set her scotch down on the red gas stove and looked at me, then shook her head as though she were a fox caught in a snare. She knew the only way out of it was to chew off her own foot. I placed one hand over my mouth, and she walked out of the house.

"It seems she's upset," he said. "Oh, Liv," he called to her. The front door creaked open but there was no sound she'd left yet. So, Rob finished. "Not a word or I can make it look like Paul was in on it too. Trust me when I say I can do that."

The hush of the door closing was like someone whimpering.

"Stop it, Rob. She had nothing to do with Larry."

"Well, I have here me..." He lifted his cell phone and fell back into his Podunk-sounding way. It was an act. "...some *di*rect evidence that she did, little missy." Then, he continued with his plan. "I can tell the spelunkers to *re*-investigate the crevice and lose evidence if I need. You know. Larry's foot could go missing too. All I really need is this." He patted the shirt pocket where he kept his phone. "You might think to impress on Liv again that if she says one word to anyone, she'll end up locked away for the rest of her life because nobody likes an author who likes to write from real life experiences. I'm not a stupid man, Jamie. Don't ever think I'm stupid."

He took another sip of his wine. Acted like he was choking a bit but was really only wanting to say something else.

"Oh, by the way, didn't I hear her say she was going to write about a man with dementia that goes missing at the library a while back? I mean, her career would be over. Like this." He snapped his fingers.

"Oh my God, Rob. Please. I'll make sure she doesn't say a word."

He cut in, "*To?*"

"What?"

"To who?" he said.

"To *anyone*. Okay?"

"Good girl. And I honestly think she'll behave."

I splashed more scotch into my glass, placed one hand on the counter and drank with the other. The liquor burned hot again and whisked away my breath.

"Easy on that. You're going to get drunk, and you never know, I might take advantage of you."

I snubbed him and polished off the scotch.

"You must be wondering why all the secrecy and fuss. I mean I could've turned you in so many times. Doesn't that bother you, even a little?"

"What do you want me to say? Huh?"

"About which, the secrecy or turning you in?"

"Good God. What do you want me to say? 'Why yes, Rob, yes. Please tell me why you are extorting us this way you mean, mean man.'"

He chuckled. "You're drunk."

"Shove it."

"Now, now. That's no way to talk to your new beau."

My mood darkened across my face. But I refused to show fear.

"That's right. That's all I want from you, Jamie. That's why.

You and I are going to be husband and wife if I have any say in the matter." He patted his pocket. "You must know how I've pined over you."

My hands began to shake. A streak of heat traveled up my back, around my neck and gripped my throat. I couldn't breathe.

As Rob spoke, he explained further. "All I want is to move in."

My mind flashed to scenes where he might have been watching her all this time. That very night, three months in between the news of Larry's foot washed up, at the morgue, on and off during these last three months, after how he showed up before the book club meeting just yesterday, how he fumbled in his pocket. Was it a ring he wanted to present to with? I glanced out the window. The sky was darker now. An indigo I used to love in cartoon movies when I was a kid. Lester cried from upstairs.

"Oh my God," I said again. "No."

He nodded the opposite, and said, "Yes."

"You took his foot?"

He looked down and chuckled. "What do you think? How else would a person have been found on the beach? It would be quite a miracle for the foot to travel from where you too dumped Larry to South Beach. Don't you think?"

I felt my stomach heave.

"Gonna get sick? Now? After what you did?"

I sipped scotch and my queasiness passed.

"Look," he said. "I don't know why you're so upset. You killed him. I mean, why hide his body if you're not guilty?"

"He fell down the stairs and broke his neck! I didn't kill him!"

"Not even a little push?" He winked.

"OhmyGod."

"Jamie, I don't care what happened. Don't you see? I've been wanting you for so many years. I've lost count of all the seasons. It was only a matter of time. But this is a fact. We're meant to be together. I mean, when I saw you two that day, I realized that this was the universe telling me that it was my chance. That I could finally have you. You're safe with me, Jamie. I love you."

I walked to the door.

"Don't you try to run," he said.

I pointed to the bathroom, raced to the door and locked myself inside.

"I can break down that door if I need," he said.

I dropped to my knees in front of the toilet. I wanted so badly to vomit but nothing came up, only a persistent stream of drool spilled out. When I stuck my finger in my mouth, I gagged and everything came up.

From outside the door, Rob said, "Well that's not the response I was hoping for." He sounded surprised, even hurt. Land in prison or try to mitigate his injured feelings? I chose to speak.

"It's only been three months."

"We could wait another three or four. Might look better."

I began to cry softly. I rested my head against the arm I had resting on the toilet seat.

I jumped when he pulled me up from behind, lifting me up by my armpits. Then, he spun me around and held me. I kept my arms by my sides.

Finally, he pulled back, bending slightly to look into my eyes. "I can pick a lock too. Especially these interior ones. Oh, Jamie. Don't you see? It's kismet, sweety."

I wrenched out of his hold and sat on the toilet. My rump slipped into the hole. He'd never have me that way. I loathed him. He disgusted me.

"Rob, how do I say this?"

"Just say it. Be brave." His smile expected a different response.

I reached up to his face. "Oh Rob," I said, "well, I just don't feel the same way."

He batted my hand away and his smile turned sinister.

He said, "Well, you better hurry up and *start* feeling the same way, and fast."

Then he threatened again. Told me that if I didn't start feeling the way he felt, even with *all* the love he had for me, he would turn me in.

"Look, Jamie." He dug inside his pant pocket. "I've been wanting to give you this for some time, now."

"No," I said.

"Hush now."

He opened his hand. In his palm was a small, black jewelry box.

I shook my head no and wiped my eyes.

"Yes. Take it. Dammit. It's the perfect thing to bind our love." He shoved it into my hand. "Open it. You'll see what I mean." He put a hand to his mouth. He enjoyed this. Was giddy. And the schoolboy demeanor returned. When I opened the small jewelry box, the shoelace that had been missing from Larry's shoe was coiled inside like a tiny, poisonous snake.

I gasped.

"By the way, why didn't you throw the foot in?"

Not Larry's foot, *the* foot.

I held a hand over my mouth and shook my head no. I may have whispered the word too. Then I pushed the box back into Rob's hands and backed away. But he caught me by the arm, wrenching my hand from my lips.

"Why?"

Tears flowed without a sound. "We thought animals...a raccoon or a fox..."

"Huh. Okay. I guess that sounds plausible. Yes. Of course. You're one smart and beautiful woman, Ms. Jamie Michaels, soon-to-be Mrs. Jamie *Rimmler*."

He pinched one end and let the lace unravel.

"I'll move in within the next six months; we'll hire someone to help. I'll put my new house back up for sale. That will help with the costs. People will suspect that after all the investigation and time we spent together that it was only natural we should become close and *fall in love*. You won't go to prison. I'll get what I want. Everyone wins."

Except everyone doesn't win. Liv was pushed to the tipping point before this. What will she do now? I worried for her sanity, for her safety, for her life.

Larry didn't win. Larry became a tool for Rob's purposes. A cog in his plan to extort me into a life spent in a metaphorical prison.

The only winner was Rob. He was the only one who got what he wanted. I wanted Larry to be alive. I wanted to grow old with him even if his mind was going. We loved each other. I had zero feelings for Rob. Because how can you truly be in love with your prison master?

SIX MONTHS
LATER—March 31, 2021

"Seeing death as the end of life is like seeing the horizon as the end of the ocean."
—David Searls

CHAPTER 36

Rob moved in.

A raven crowing somewhere in the bank of firs outside the window woke me early this morning. It warned me to get up for work but also scurry out of bed in time to avoid Rob's reaching hands.

The "second-story garden" in the gutters had grown worse from the wet winter and an early warm spring. It was still edged with plants from seeds finding their homes there, that had taken root and sprouted.

Before I rose, however, I allowed my eyes to travel outside the window next to my side of the bed. The day was burgeoning, clear and bright. The digital clock read 6:35, later than normal but what was normal these days? Nothing. Certainly not my sleeping, rising multiple times throughout the night. Rest escaped me. A strange man in your bed will do that. But for whatever reason, I got a solid two hours from the last time I arose.

The sun was piercing and warm on my face, on the pillow. Its glow showing me a path. But a path to where?

From my angular, upside-down view, higher along the eave, one of many growing sprigs poked its nagging head high above the gutter, a yard higher. I imagined it with its leafy hands on its swaying hips taunting me saying, *Neener neener neener! You can't hurt me!* Like a bully taunting another child he'd pushed down into a sandbox.

But the bully was wrong. I knew I could take him.

I rolled up into a sitting position on the bed and in an instant felt Rob close in next to me.

The warmth of his hand dragged at the crook of my elbow. I wriggled out of his grip. And holding onto the skin where he'd touched me, my skin prickled.

Lester had taken up rent on his hips and thighs. The cat had switched loyalties. Animals are like that. They understand pecking order far better than humans. Animals don't need someone to tell them that they're in charge now. They sense a takeover. No need to explain anything with animals.

"I need to get up," I said. "Lester loves you." It was a diversionary tactic but with Rob's training, it didn't dissuade him.

"When will we, Jamie? It's been weeks since I moved in."

I shifted on the bed to face him better. A mix of sadness and anger flashed over his face, he fell back onto his pillow and placed one arm over his eyes. I shifted away, my eyes falling onto the marble of the bathroom floor.

"I want to get busy early. I accidentally slept late."

"There's always an excuse."

"Look. I can't stand looking at the gutters anymore. I need to do it today."

He blew air out in resignation. I stood.

"Fine," he said, his voice edgy with anger.

"Hey. Look," I said again, "How 'bout this? After, I'll take a shower 'cause it's a real dirty job. Then...well, we'll have the rest of the day..."

His eyes filled with hope.

"I can help." He threw off his blankets, irritating Lester and making him scramble off and onto the thick comforter that lay across the end of the bed. After lying down on its softness, Lester seemed happy again.

I told Rob to stay in bed. Because, I'd said, "it's only six-thirty."

I cleaned my teeth, dragged a brush though my hair pulling it into a scrunchy, then slipped on a headband.

I stood in the closet deciding what to wear this time. I usually was a better planner but not this morning. You don't plan things like this. I guess. Sometimes things like this are sudden and take on a life of their own.

I miss you, Larry.

I tugged on a pair of baggy sweatpants, a sloppy tee shirt, and a zip-up gray jacket that was loose but matched my sweats. What would Rob know? He had no frame of reference when it came to cleaning the gutters. Anyway, I didn't want him gawking at my frame if I were to wear the requisite, tighter clothing.

As I headed out the master bedroom—*mine and Larry's* bedroom—Rob called out, "Don't forget that tether you told me about." Almost as if he had intuited that I would forget. I could hear him tugging on the pants he'd worn yesterday, a pair of mustard jeans he'd slung over the wooden bench at the foot of the bed.

And when was it that I had told him? Conversations with Rob evaporated in the mist for me. For him, each word I spoke he held as cherished, something to tuck away in a locket, much the way I held conversations with Larry—even on that last day when, as he began to fall, he called out, "Help me," he'd said. "Help me, Jamie!" Those were his exact words, words that indict me all day, all night, in my dreams.

And I don't know if it was because I was tired of taking care of people by then, taking care of Larry—of the dirty diapers, the daily medicine, picking up wet towels off the bathroom floor, washing him when he had accidents. Or, if I was afraid for my own safety—that he would drag me down the stairs with him if he fell.

But my actions, after he needed me before falling to his death, haunt me.

I pulled my hands out of his reach. I shrank against the wall and turned my head, so I didn't have to watch him fall.

I might've saved him, probably could have diverted him away from the stairs, but I didn't even try. I turned from Larry. I let him go.

Rob called to me again. Something about breakfast. Eggs, maybe. He walked to the landing and looked down on me. I left the door open midway and Lester darted out. I didn't try to stop him. What was the point?

"Hey," I said to Rob. "Thanks for allowing me some time to get my head wrapped around all of this."

He made his way down to me. His smile made me want to vomit.

"Cats out," he said.

"He'll come back."

I faked it. Grabbed him around the waist and pulled him into a hug. He didn't seem to know where to put his arms, then, accepting my hug, placed them over my shoulders and squeezed. While he squeezed, I slipped his handkerchief out of his back pocket. Always there. Always there. And balled it into my fist, pulled out of our embrace, and turned back toward the door.

When I stepped outside, I turned back and gave him a look that I would describe as the intersection between happy and sad.

He called out something about a glass of champagne to celebrate our *consummation*, he said. Rob wasn't what I would call a "word guy" but somehow managed to pull out the word *consummation* from some wrinkle in his devious brain.

The day was warm for March. So warm that ravens were already busy yelling, barking at one another. One big boy flew overhead in a complete circle on my walk out to the barn. It spread open its wide black wings and floated down, alighting on the frontmost ridge of barn, but he hopped back as I approached him and flew away when I got too close.

I pulled off my jacket and tied it in a loose knot around my waist. I left my belt and tethers on their hook inside the barn and headed back to the house carrying my handy-dandy, commercial-grade, aluminum extendable ladder. It clanked with each step lugging it to the back of the house. I placed it up onto the back deck where, from bed, I spotted the annoying growth in the gutter, and angled the ladder just so, a few feet away from the house so that if I leaned awkwardly, I wouldn't fall backward.

After setting the angle perfectly, I climbed to the top, lifted my leg up and over the gutter, and stepped easily onto the roof.

It was mossier back here. After taking in the entirety of the job—a fifteen-hundred-foot span of red composite tile mixed in a patchwork of moss, I walked back to the ladder. The gas barbecue still had its plastic cover over it, speckled in pollen from two years of nonuse. Two Adirondack chairs were still flipped over, something I'd done to prevent water from etching out the teak seats. A thin, leafless wisteria sat in its pot against a trellis, sure to sprout and put on a show by June.

My heart ached. Despair is like that. Like a papercut on the knuckle constantly busting open and refusing to heal. Grief is different in its pain. In time, grief gets tucked away into secret compartments of your heart that you can later choose from to pull out and look at so that you don't forget. But despair...no. It runs through your veins like diseased blood.

I shut my eyes, taking in the scent of the overgrown mock orange. Even its leaves smelled good, steaming in an earthy scent. And between the aroma of orange blossom and hearing the raven crowing, crowing, crowing, I let my body loosen, aware for only a second the effect of gravity pulling my weight, a split-second prayer asking God's forgiveness for giving up, aware that Rob might have seen me fall, certainly hopeful he did, aware of a single gasp and a snapping bone in my neck, envisioning Larry standing with his arms out before me, catching me in that last breath, and before finally letting the light spill from my eyes.

The Chronicler of the San Juan Islands
Published 8:12 AM PDT, April 1, 2021
LONG-TIME RESIDENT DIES

SAN JUAN COUNTY, Wash.—Long-time resident of Friday Harbor, Jamie Michaels, 51, was found dead outside her home early yesterday morning in what is being called an "apparent accident."

"Michaels fell from the roof and sustained fatal injuries after breaking her neck," said Sheriff Bill Klem.

However, authorities stated that foul play had not yet been ruled out.

In his statement, Klem told reporters that a witness had come forward which, he said, "complicated matters." The witness and Michaels were being extorted by a person of interest about the death of Michaels' husband, who had gone missing in June 2020. He also added, "We're looking in to see if the Michaels incident and the Afon Colling murder are connected."

Klem stated that because of these complications, a wider investigation is underway.

AFTERWORD

As I write this novel, I feel compelled to explain a few things...

I've taken some freedoms regarding island facts. Such as, the San Juan County Coroner's Office doesn't have a morgue. All pathologies are shipped and examined off-island on the mainland. There is no huge crevice on our property. And most importantly, Bob, my husband is still alive and well. Thank God.

I've set some of the action on days that coincide with my husband, Bob's birthday, which is June 20th. I'm writing this story in 2020 and we just celebrated his 73rd birthday. So, yes. Bob is alive and well at the writing of this fictional tale. And we celebrated his birthday with the usual gift-giving, special dinner and cake. The 21st was Father's Day. His son called and made Bob's eyes fill with tears of joy.

His youngest daughter called too. Again, he got emotional but talked with her more than he did with Mike because they've had more time together.

And in between those calls from his kids, we mowed the lawn. A great Father's Day activity, don't you think? But one that exhausted Bob. The following is my attempt to explain some important history about our family.

Those who may not know me all that well will be better informed by the fact that from June of 2015 to December of 2016 my mother lived with us. Doctors diagnosed her medical condition as COPD—Chronic Obstructive Pulmonary Disease in

2003. On June 10th, when she was whisked away to the hospital in Bellingham, Washington. We live on San Juan Island in Washington State, so I had to make a few trips off-island to visit but the docs there said, if she doesn't quit smoking, she'll be dead in five to ten years. She didn't quit smoking until 2007 when they put her on oxygen. By 2010, my mother began showing signs of mental decline—hallucinations, paranoia, the inability to properly care for herself or her cat and dog, an incapacity to clean her house or feed herself well. I say *well* because she existed, I now know, for several years on hamburger patties and ice cream bars. By 2015, when she finally moved in with us, Mom was completely incapable of caring for herself. It took four months to after we moved her into our home for me to understand. I was distracted by her violent outbursts, anger and hallucinations. Another story entirely.

Fast forward to 2017 and six months after my mom died…

Bob began showing problems with word-finding. He'd told me once while we were prepping for Mom's move in with us that he felt like he had Alzheimer's. He'd said it in reference to one of Mom's diagnoses. I pish-poshed Bob's concerns away. My sister, Lizz was helping us fix up the attached studio apartment where Mom would live. Between all my concerns about Mom's segue into our home, I had little capacity for anyone else's problems. Certainly not Bob's and certainly not another case of Alzheimer's.

So, after Mom died, with his word-finding issue—getting those words off his tongue—we decided to contact a neurologist who did some tests and who ultimately sent Larry to see a neuropsychologist. The neuropsychologist diagnosed Bob with Aphasia. But what she and the neurologist did not diagnose was the underlying cause of the Aphasia which we now know is dementia, frontotemporal dementia, to be exact.

The reason I'm explaining all Bob's and Mom's sicknesses is because in writing this novel, *When You Leave Me*, I decided to blend both my Mom's and Bob's symptoms together. Both suffered similar problems at times. However, most often, my mother's symptoms exhibited far worse than Bob's. The reason? Bob's physical health isn't nearly as critical as my mother's was. Her physical health was in rapid decline by the time she moved in because of the COPD. I mean, without oxygen getting into those lungs of hers, little if any oxygen got into her blood. And as most of us know, if no oxygen in the blood, there's none getting to the brain. She was extremely frail and sick.

For Bob, it's opposite. He looks healthy and, at the completion of the writing of *When You Leave Me* could still push our new electric lawnmower around, albeit with a little help from me holding the electrical cord as he goes. But still...

He eats well, walks a little, and he's happy and sweet. Still, he has heart issues and because of those heart issues, he has oxygen issues which means mental decline, which means he cannot have a desperately needed heart operation because of the mental decline and the wheel goes round and round.

They gave him five to seven years mid-2019 and I count the minutes with a sense of gratefulness but also with dread. I don't want my husband to die. I'm heartbroken that he has dementia because if he didn't, we could get his heart repaired. I go round and round on this ugly wheel almost daily. And daily, I end up heartbroken by the fact that we're playing a waiting game. My heart goes out to others in similar circumstances, to those who have been diagnosed with terminal illnesses, and to their families and friends. It's the worst wait imaginable.

I'm not sure if Bob remembers the doctor's prognosis about his life expectation. I think he might, but hope the dementia deleted that information from his databank. Because, as I prayed for my mom, I don't want him to be afraid. I don't want him to worry that today might be *the* day. I just want him to live and be happy, even if we only have a few more years together, I want to revel in those years and keep each moment as close to my heart as possible.

Which brings me to this story, *When You Leave Me*. It began as a charting of the progress of Bob's health issues caused by dementia but soon spun into a fictional tale.

And for those people who might be going through a similar experience and who are caring for a loved one with dementia or Alzheimer's, I say this: Forgive yourself of your thoughts. Forgive yourself of tomorrow. Forgive yourself of things you think you did wrong and cannot change. You only have today. Cherish today.

God bless us all.

—Susan Wingate

ACKNOWLEDGMENTS

Usually, no sooner do I finish one novel, I turn around and start another. Stories come fast and furious. Not after this one. Because the story hits so close to home, with Bob's dementia in what, if you read the online literature about the disease, he appears to be in stage six moving into stage seven.

Glenn, one of his best friends, came up not long ago. He said, "I was looking at ALZ.org and reading through the stages. You said he's in six moving into seven." Then, he paused and when he did, I said, "Yes." Then he added, "There's no stage eight."

It was a heartbreaking admission, his realization that his best buddy would be alive, if the experts were correct, no more than five years. So, first I want to acknowledge all of Bob's best friends—Glenn, Jim B., Jim C., Greg, Johnny, and Ralph—for their undying dedication to visits and talks, for simply being faces on the other side of Skype chats or in person. Although he's mostly silent, I can see how happy you make him. You see, it's all in his blue eyes, his joy lives in those eyes.

I want to thank everyone at Down & Out Books for their expertise and commitment to detail with editing but also with help marketing. Thank you to Rachel Anderson at RMA Publicity who can pull rabbits out of hats. To Chip MacGregor who fell in love with Jamie Michaels's story. This story might never have seen the light of day if not for you. Thank you for your constant support and willingness to let free the wild horses running through my heart and mind.

To my tag team, Jenni Gold and Terry Persun. Our sort-of-weekly writer chats are the highlight of my week.

To Joshua Graham, my brother in Christ. You're a shining example of what goodness looks like.

To my dear friend, Kim, who without the emails from her various cats, life would be so dull.

To my dear friend, Carol. You never disappoint. I love our phone wine chats, our discussions about aging kitties, and all the giggles too.

To everyone at The Little Store who keep the business afloat. Without you, Bob's baby wouldn't be. You're the reason the doors are still open.

To this island. God, I love this place.

To Bob's kids: he loves you more than life itself.

To Bob's brothers: he often sees your spirit brother these days. Time is of the essence.

To my sister who ran after me with a hanger when I got her in trouble and then who got in trouble again because she was running after me with a hanger...we were terrible kids. We owe Mom and Dad a big apology when we see them again in Heaven.

Mostly, I want to say "thank you" to the man who changed my life but who cannot read words anymore and can barely say any. I love you more than breathing. More than waking. I wish it were me instead of you. I worry day and night that if anything would happen to me, what would happen to Bob? A torment no one should ever bear. I will love you to the end of the universe and back. I will love you for eternity. Thank you for choosing me, for choosing us. Thank you for being my best friend ever.

The journey has been awesome. I wouldn't have it any other way.

SUSAN WINGATE writes about big trouble in small towns and lives with her husband on an island off the coast of Washington State where, against State laws, she feeds the wildlife because she wants them to follow her. Her ukulele playing is (as her Sitto used to say) coming along.

Susan Wingate is a #1 Amazon bestselling and award-winning author. Her story "How the Deer Moon Hungers" has won seven book awards, including a first-place award in the 2020 Chanticleer Somerset Awards, a Silver Award in the 2021 eLit Book Awards, the 2020 SABA Book Awards for the Judge's Selection "Best Fiction Author," Best Fiction in the 2020 Pacific Book Award, a Silver Award in the 2020 Moonbeam Children's Book Award, and July 2020 Book Cover in the Book Cover of the Month Awards.

BOOKS

On the following pages are a few
more great titles from the
Down & Out Books publishing family.

For a complete list of books and to
sign up for our newsletter,
go to DownAndOutBooks.com.

Bad Guy Lawyer
Chuck Marten

Down & Out Books
March 2022
978-1-64396-249-8

The only time Guy McCann stops talking is when he's downing scotch. Guy was a hot-shot attorney for the West Coast mafia until he got cold feet and split town, earning a target on his head. Now he's lying low in Las Vegas, giving back-room legal advice to second-rate crooks while pining over his old girlfriend Blair, a working girl with a razor wit and zero inhibitions.

When Blair is committed to a psychiatric ward, Guy is drawn back to the dangerous underworld of Los Angeles. Next thing he knows, Blair has escaped from the hospital and Guy's former mafia associates are on her trail, with Guy caught in the cross-fire.

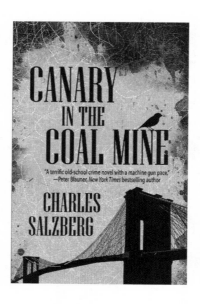

Canary in the Coal Mine
Charles Salzberg

Down & Out Books
April 2022
978-1-64396-251-1

Pete Fortunato, a NYC PI who suffers from anger management issues and insomnia, is hired by a beautiful woman to find her husband.

When he finds him shot dead in the apartment of her young boyfriend, this is the beginning of a nightmare as he's chased by the Albanian mob sending him half-way across the country in an attempt to find missing money which can save his life.

The Damned Lovely
Adam Frost

Down & Out Books
May 2022
978-1-64396-253-5

"She wasn't pretty but she was ours…" Sandwiched between seedy businesses in the scorching east LA suburb of Glendale, the Damned Lovely dive bar is as scarred as its regulars: ex-cops, misfits and loners. And for Sam Goss, it's a refuge from the promising life he's walked away from, a place to write and a hole to hide in.

But when a beautiful and mysterious new patron to the bar turns up murdered as the third victim of a serial killer terrorizing the local streets, Sam can't stop himself from getting involved. Despite their fleeting interaction, or perhaps because of it, something about her ghost won't let go…

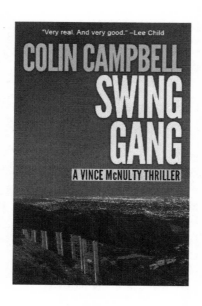

Swing Gang
A Vince McNulty Thriller
Colin Campbell

Down & Out Books
June 2022
978-1-64396-268-9

Titanic Productions has moved to Hollywood but the producer's problems don't stop with the cost of location services.

When McNulty finds a runaway girl hiding at the Hollywood Boulevard location during a night shoot e takes the girl under his wing but she runs away again.

Between the drug cartel that wants her back and a hitman who wants her dead, McNulty must find her again before California wildfires race towards her hiding place.

Made in the USA
Columbia, SC
23 July 2022